What the critics are saying…

5 *Hearts* "I love both of these authors and when they collaborate, they are even better." ~ *Maura Frankman The Romance Studio*

"*Red Light Specialists* is a super sexy series of adventures featuring three tough, beautiful women who are highly trained special agents…With gorgeous alpha males in settings that range from an ancient royal harem, a cursed jungle temple to a futuristic casino, each woman's story is entertaining and different. The sexuality is explicit, adventurous and arousing with each couple finding that their passions are ignited on first sight. But M&M also infuse each situation and character with humor as well as lusty satisfaction. This is a fine start to an exciting new paranormal series!" ~ *Patrice Storie ~ Just Erotic Romance Reviews*

"The formidable duo of M&M has done it again. *Ms. Roth* and *Ms. Pillow's* unique rapport shines through their characters. Each of these ladies have impressive writing careers and together they sizzle the pages…When these ladies let loose with their men expect the temperature to rise." ~ *Jodi Romance Junkies*

"Both authors are very talented in their own right and together, it was a sure thing that they would pen a hot, erotic, highly entertaining story." ~ *Valerie Love Romances*

"I hope that *Ms. Pillow* and *Ms. Roth* have more collaborations on the horizon." ~ *Susan Biliter EcataRomance Reviews*

MANDY M. ROTH
MICHELLE M. PILLOW

Michelle m Pillow

Red Light
SPECIALISTS

ELLORA'S CAVE
ROMANTICA PUBLISHING

An Ellora's Cave Romantica Publication

www.ellorascave.com

Red Light Specialists

ISBN # 1419953095
ALL RIGHTS RESERVED.
Red Light Specialists
Copyright© 2005 Michelle M. Pillow & Mandy M. Roth
Edited by: Briana St. James
Cover art by: Syneca

Electronic book Publication: June, 2005
Trade paperback Publication: December, 2005

Excerpt from *Pleasure Cruise*
 Copyright © Mandy M. Roth and Michelle M. Pillow 2005

Warning:

The following material contains graphic sexual content meant for mature readers. *Red Light Specialists* has been rated *E-rotic* by a minimum of three independent reviewers.

Ellora's Cave Publishing offers three levels of Romantica™ reading entertainment: S (S-ensuous), E (E-rotic), and X (X-treme).

S-*ensuous* love scenes are explicit and leave nothing to the imagination.

E-*rotic* love scenes are explicit, leave nothing to the imagination, and are high in volume per the overall word count. In addition, some E-rated titles might contain fantasy material that some readers find objectionable, such as bondage, submission, same sex encounters, forced seductions, etc. E-rated titles are the most graphic titles we carry; it is common, for instance, for an author to use words such as "fucking", "cock", "pussy", etc., within their work of literature.

X-*treme* titles differ from E-rated titles only in plot premise and storyline execution. Unlike E-rated titles, stories designated with the letter X tend to contain controversial subject matter not for the faint of heart.

Red Light Specialists

Part One
Agent Selection

Chapter One

*Restigatio Women's Correctional Facility, RLS-69 Agent
Headquarters*

Simon Thornton glanced up at the large rectangular viewing screen, which expanded the full length of one pale gray office wall, and bit back a chuckle. "Abbi, what in the universe are you trying to do?"

"I'm counting." The image of the raven-haired beauty twisted once more. This time she bent forward, exposing the soft, tanned globes of her ass cheeks to him. Was he mistaken, or did he see her...?

Simon swallowed uncomfortably as his cock hardened, forcing him to adjust in his seat. He had to remind himself that Abbi wasn't real. She was just another form of artificial intelligence that he and his associates had spent centuries developing. Still, it didn't stop him from taking another peek as she made little bounces in her alluring position.

Normal A.I. could only be based off human intelligence. Their advanced versions were able to stand on platforms not related to humans. The name Abbi actually stood for two things. The first of which was Artificial Broad Based Intelligence. The second meaning behind her name was personal to Simon and was discussed with no one. Not even the closest of his RLS agents.

Oh, but what a piece of work Abbi was. With her long legs, tiny waist, large breasts and heart-shaped face, she took Simon's breath away daily. That was unexpected, considering he'd been the one to set the A.I.'s image up. He'd spent months programming in every minute detail, sculpting her into what he considered to be the most beautiful woman in the universe.

As much as he wanted to take all the credit in the creativity department, he couldn't. Abbi was modeled after a woman he'd not only known but had loved dearly. That was how he came up with every tiny detail on her body and how he'd gotten her to look so lifelike—down to the thin scar on her upper thigh. Granted, she was only an image on a computer screen, but she "felt" real to him. And he'd done a relatively good job in the A.I.'s personality department as well. Not perfect, but good all the same.

What could he say? A man had to have a hobby—especially when surrounded by toned female agents every day. It was either that or he would spend all of his time concentrating on how hard his dick was rather than working on something productive.

"No, Abbi," Simon took a deep breath, unable to take his eyes away from her as she stretched her arms to the side and twisted at the waist. With each turn, he saw a delectable view of her large breasts. Suppressing a groan, he asked, "What are you *doing*?"

Abbi glanced his way, her head almost hitting the floor as she touched her toes. "I observed Agent Trinity working out this morning and I wished to see what the appeal was. She seems to enjoy it."

Simon again had to bite back a laugh. Why ever did he program Abbi to act so human? To be so curious that she actually mimicked the other women? "I see. Well, was agent Trinity exercising nude?"

"Yes. She spends the majority of her time in her quarters nude. Many of the RLS-69s do not wear clothing while alone." Abbi paused in her movement, striking an absurdly seductive pose as she was leaning halfway over. Her body angled slightly toward him, but away. She tossed her hair over her back and tilted her head to the side to look at him. "I have also noticed that all of the women on the planet look similar—like actual Earthlings. Only a few have any attributes of alien races and even those are barely noticeable."

As she said the words, flashes of naked body parts came on the viewing screen next to her. The photographs were close-ups of the different alien features the women had — violet cat-shaped eyes, an extra-long tongue, a blue tribal birthmark spanning across a flat stomach. Simon took a deep breath at the last one. The scrolling design dipped really low on the hips, touching the top of the agent's hairless pussy. More images flashed, but he barely looked at them. He was trying too hard to will his erection down.

"They all appear to be humanoids," Abbi continued, completely unaware of the increasing discomfort of his growing erection.

"They are all humanoids, Abbi, even the humans. Humans are those from Earth. Humanoids are any alien species compatible to mating with human DNA."

"I know that, Simon," Abbi said, affecting a small pout. Simon hid his smile behind his hand. He'd only explained it to her out of habit. Abbi was programmed to learn and he'd been the one teaching her since she was first switched on. Only now, she was getting more independent. "What I was trying to say is that it will no doubt come into question as to why we have so many *human-looking* humanoids and not other kinds. How am I to address this?"

To his relief, the images of close-up body parts stopped. However, the feeling was short-lived as he saw Abbi was still posed, her perfect body arched in such a way as to drive any man mad. Had she been real, he would've thought she did it on purpose. As it was, he knew she had no knowledge of the effect her naked form had on him.

"I take it that outside sources have attempted to access our recorder databases again." Simon let out a soft sigh. "Were you able to deny access to them?"

Abbi nodded and stood. She continued her cyber workout, reaching toward the ceiling with little bouncing stretches. "Yes. However, the attacks are becoming increasingly more aggressive. It would seem many species are curious about the inmates of the Restigatio Correctional Facility. The security cameras outside of the general population's shower complex seem to be a favorite target, though many of the main complex's recorders are being hit on a daily basis as well. Deductive reasoning has led me to the conclusion that you should issue a general statement to the media. I have created a folder containing photos of the main complex along with that of the surrounding area. No girls have been included as of yet and I would assume that you would rather not incorporate any of the RLS facilities or our agents in the file."

"No, this facility needs to remain a secret. Just send pictures of the main prison complex. No one needs to know this building even exists." Simon leaned back a bit. "The fact that our agents' identities stay hidden is key to their survival. Speak with the warden and arrange for a large group of women to be pulled from the general population. Photos can be taken as they go along with their normal routines."

A scrolling marquee of his directive appeared in the lower left corner of the viewing screen, verifying that Abbi had not only received the order but was processing it as well. "Simon, how would you have me address the lack of other humanoid and non-humanoid life-forms within the prison system?"

"That's an easy one." Simon tapped a black button on his desk and waited for a keypad to push toward him. Placing his long fingers on it, he began the process of inputting the data Abbi would need to handle the situation. "Access this file whenever needed. It reiterates 4C83.b from the detaining bylaws set forth twelve years ago. While it's ignored by ninety-nine percent of the universe, we are adhering to it."

Abbi winked. "Ah, yes, the section that deals with the universe's dislike of Earth culture. How, in order to provide a safe facility in accordance with the rules and regulations on correctional institutions inmates' safety and liability section 1G36.1, it is highly suggested that all humans and human-hybrids be held separate from the general universal population of offenders, since many alien species blame all such humanoids for what the ancient Earth humans did. You are a brilliant man, Simon."

"I don't know about brilliant, Abbi," he mused as he saved the form letter to the proper location and closed the keypad. "I'm just resourceful. Our project requires those with trace amounts of human DNA and the clause is there. It makes sense to take advantage of it. We can plug ourselves as providing a much needed service. Aliens have countless other facilities spread across the universe. We currently have only one dedicated to humans. In fact, they might appreciate having a place to send such humanoids so they don't have to deal with them in their populations."

Abbi beamed as she smiled at Simon. She stood before him naked, her lush curves drawing his eyes down her body. Abbi didn't notice, saying, "I've added the letter of explanation to the press release folder. As soon as I've assembled the rest of the required data, I will run it by you for final approval."

"Perfect."

Abbi went back to her workout, again bending over. "Now, do you wish for me to calculate the percentage of RLS agents that prefer to walk around nude when alone? I can assess my records if you like."

"Um, no, Abbi, that's fine," he answered, though her comment did pique Simon's interest. It had been a long time since he'd known the comforts of a female and he was very interested in seeing more about this development. However, staring at Abbi's naked ass spread wide before him, even if only on a monitor, was too much. "Abbi, please dress yourself."

She stood quickly and nodded. "Yes, Simon."

Instantly, she was dressed in a short red miniskirt and a tight black T-shirt. It wasn't exactly what he had in mind but it would do. What he had in mind was a turtleneck and baggy pants. Then and only then he might actually be able to focus on his job, instead of imagining different ways of burying his cock to the hilt in Abbi. Too bad he didn't have the technology to make her a real girl.

Shifting slightly in his chair, he rolled his eyes. His suit jacket suddenly felt a little too hot and his dick was so hard. It would take hours for the erection to go down of its own accord. Coming from a superhuman race of Earthlings had many advantages, or disadvantages depending on how he looked at it. Sexual stamina was definitely one of those. Lately, it seemed to be more of a curse than anything else and Abbi's little workout routine hadn't helped. Perhaps that was because he wasn't getting sex as often as he would like, or really at all—unless he counted his hand as full-blown intercourse. He didn't.

"I can't walk around with a stiff one all day." He again shifted his hips. It didn't help.

"A stiff what, Simon?"

"Never mind." Freeing his cock from his dark gray slacks, he kept it hidden beneath his long black desk. The furniture spanned the wall beneath the large viewing screen. Its slight curve helped to hide his lower region from view of both guests and Abbi. He really didn't want her asking questions about why his dick was hard and why he needed to touch it. It didn't take long for him to change his mind about seeing the naked agents. Trying to keep his voice level, he asked, "Are there any agents naked now?"

"Yes, Simon." Abbi paced back and forth on the screen, tapping her chin in thought. "My calculations indicate that there are at least two completely naked agents in the RLS facility at all times."

Simon looked up at Abbi and fisted his cock. He stroked it a few times, suppressing a moan. She was oblivious to his masturbating, as always. He ran his fingers over the head of his cock and then brought them to his mouth. Lathering them with saliva, he nodded to Abbi. His tone hoarse, he said, "Show me a view of one of the agents who is naked at the present moment. Preferably one who is in the process of seeking pleasure."

"Seeking pleasure?"

"Stimulating their reproductive organs, Abbi."

"Yes, Simon." Abbi paused. "There are currently fifty-nine agents in the facility seeking pleasure, but not all of them are completely nude."

"Ah, just give me a blonde," Simon snapped, frustrated. *Fifty-nine?*

"Currently there are twenty-eight blondes seeking—"

"Abbi," Simon interrupted a little too brusquely. Masturbation had never been so hard. Trying to calm his voice, he exhaled. "Just give me the one whose first letter of the first name is closest to the beginning of the human English alphabet you were just studying."

Instantly, the screen split. An image of agent Bianca appeared on one side. She was a sexy little blonde with an ass any man would want to sink his cock into. Simon ran his fist over his hard shaft several times as he checked her out. She was alone in her quarters. Her tight body was a product of working in the stone mines all day.

Restigatio, the correctional planet they all resided on, housed convicted criminals from at least three galaxies. There was talk of expanding its system even further and Simon hoped the rumors were true. Even though he didn't agree with ninety percent of the charges the women were convicted for, he and his people would benefit too much from it to protest.

Besides, it wasn't wise for his people, the *figiutatio*, to expose themselves in high-profile disputes. Being immortal meant that he'd not only been alive during a time when the rest of the universe turned on Earth, but he'd been one of the men who'd tried to stop the planet's destruction during the Cleansing Wars centuries ago. After the war the *figiutatio* hid among the various humanoid cultures in the universe. Luckily, many humans had done the same, surviving by blending in and reproducing with compatible humanoid species. Aside from his kind, there were few full-blooded humans left.

It wasn't as though he should've cared what happened to the "normal humans" from Earth. No. The humans had turned their backs on his kind and hunted them for close to a hundred years prior to the start of the Cleansing Wars. But Earth had been his people's home regardless of what had gone on there. Even if the *figiutatio* wanted to denounce their Earth heritage, they couldn't deny the fact that they needed to mate with those who carried human DNA. In the end it was the same as being an Earth supporter and there was little point in siding with the universe.

Without humans, no matter how cruel some could be, the *figiutatio* would be alone. No mates. No one to love, to hold, to have a family with. It was a harsh reality. One he and the others like him had learned to cope with centuries before.

The *figiutatio* had been the next phase of evolution for the Earthlings. They'd been slow in coming and for many centuries wrongly labeled as demons. Normal humans had reacted with violence toward them, mostly out of their ignorance, taking the lives of many of his people. Some were burned at the stake. Others were hunted, beheaded, shot with silver bullets or impaled through the heart.

Long ago, the humans of Earth were known for exploiting any weakness they could find. They treated the supernatural creatures as separate entities, yet assumed they'd all spawned from the fires of hell. While some did, others did not. The *figiutatio* encompassed all walks of supernatural creatures—vampires, lycans, witches, sorcerers and countless other creatures. What made them different is that they were pure bloods, ancients, masters amongst their races. It wasn't until the Cleansing Wars that the "supernatural" realized they needed to band together and stop segregating themselves. Unfortunately, it was already too late.

Simon continued to stroke his cock as he watched the screen but didn't actually see it. "Ah, I miss the days when our numbers were strong and our people were proud."

He missed the days when he could pleasure himself and not have other thoughts invading his mind, when release was met with mindless abandonment.

"If you are referring to the *figiutatio*, you are still proud and resourceful."

Hearing Abbi turn his early words back at him in a manner that suited the conversation made Simon smile. She'd come a long way in the A.I. department and he knew she'd go even further. "Thanks, Abbi. I needed that."

"Soon the rest of the universe will understand just how powerful the *figiutatio* are, Simon. It stands to reason that they believe you are all a myth." She gave him a questioning look. "Are you well? Does your leg itch?"

Does my leg itch?

Simon let out a soft laugh as he realized that Abbi was referring to his hand moving under the desk. No. His leg didn't itch. His cock ached to find relief in the solace of her body. Since that was physically impossible, Simon would have to settle for handling matters himself—just as he had to handle matters concerning the repopulation of his race by himself for so many years. That was until he'd finally reunited with several old friends.

The very fact that Simon and his associates were now ready to embark on a mission they'd spent nearly two hundred years organizing was ironic. The mission's goal was to not only save their species, which was dying off at an alarming rate, but to save the human lineage as well. Ironically, they were saving the very thing that had tried to kill them off to begin with.

Over the centuries many of Earth's survivors had mated with humanoids on other planets, thus thinning the amount of human blood in their lineage. Simon and his associates were happy to know that many humans had managed to blend in on whatever planet they happened to inhabit. However, there were those that didn't assimilate as well into the other cultures. It was those, the ones with more human DNA, that the *figiutatio* had a better chance of mating with. For agents that held only a small amount of human DNA, their mates would be found in various places. Many would even end up with those Earth had once regarded as enemies. Now, so many centuries later, the fences needed to be mended and hopefully, the project would do just that. "Simon, do you wish me to close the viewing screen now?" Abbi asked, startling him.

He blinked and focused on the screen before him. "Umm, no, Abbi. Leave it open please."

Simon couldn't stop his tongue from flickering out and over his lower lip as he watched the sight before him. Bianca was one of the prisoners Simon had hand selected from the completely female population of inmates on Restigatio. Not all the prisoners in general population would do. One of his almost endless powers was that of foresight. Another was the ability to sense traces of human in someone. Still another was his ability to see into one's heart. While these powers were not exclusively his, Simon did have a greater grasp on them than any other *figiutatio* he'd met to date. These were also the weakest of his gifts, which meant he was one hell of a powerful man. It was a fact he was not only aware of but one he wished he could change. It was part of the reason he'd lost the love of his life.

When the enemy wants to strike out and make the biggest impact, they strike out at the strongest leader they can find. Sometimes, they miss their target but end up doing more damage than they originally set out to.

Don't visit the past now. It will only leave you hurting for months to come.

Not wanting to dwell on things that could not be changed, Simon focused on Bianca. She'd been convicted on minor gambling charges and sentenced to a life on Restigatio. Her home planet took debt seriously and Bianca had amassed enough of it to land her before the majesty. The moment she'd set foot on the planet, he'd sensed the minute bit of human blood in her. She was unaware of this, of course, and that was fine. She need not understand all the details of her family line.

The only thing she needed to do was meet her soul mate and aid in the repopulation of humans.

Simon knew exactly who Bianca's mate was and smiled at the irony of it all. She, like many of the women who had been selected for this mission, was destined for an important figurehead of a planet that had played a significant role in the destruction of Earth and its population centuries before. In no way could these men be held accountable for the actions of their ancestors, as the remaining humans could not be either.

The figureheads would play key roles in the future of the repopulation plans Simon had. Without their help, the next generation of humans, *figiutatio* or not, wouldn't survive. The target on all humans had remained intact for centuries, causing humans to live in shame of their heritage. Bringing children into the universe without ample protection from the powerful planets was the same as sentencing them to death. That was not acceptable.

When Simon had discovered that many of the key players in the destruction of Earth had men in positions of power that were destined to mate with humanoids, he could barely contain himself. Love does amazing things to people. Hopefully, the agents whose soul mates were from this selection of men would be able to help their mates see the need to protect not only their offspring but that of any other humanoids as well.

Holding humans accountable for the greed of ancient Earthlings was insane. The ones who lived today had no part in their ancestors' sins. The ancient Earthlings had attempted colonization of every galaxy in a four-hundred light-year radius, and in the process they had destroyed entire species to control resources. The humans now simply existed. That was all. Although everyone knew that the ancient Earth government had been the ones calling the shots, Earth's enemies still took it out on the innocent human race. The actions of a few had cost the lives of many.

Stop dwelling on events you know will occur if you play your cards right and start focusing on the gorgeous woman before you.

Simon gave in to his inner voice and glanced at the viewing screen. Bianca was on her bed staring up at the ceiling. Even this far away from her, Simon could sense her loneliness. All of his girls were lonely. It was par for the course on Restigatio. He was one of the only men, aside from the guards and the warden, and he made it a rule to never sleep with his agents. The temptation to break his own rule was great, but to do so could mean interfering with what the fates had decided long ago. If he were to fuck one of his agents and she became pregnant or, worse yet, mistook the sex for love, then it would mean that she would not meet her true soul mate. While that sounded minor, the results could be catastrophic. The fates determined things for a reason and their methods were a mystery even to Simon.

Thoughts of sex left Simon burning with the need to find release even though he knew it was next to impossible. Shifting in the seat slightly, he pushed his pants down a bit more, freeing his cock completely.

Simon pumped his cock and used his free hand to massage his balls. Gods, how he missed the touch of a woman, the feel of release. Giving in would be so easy. Repairing the potential damage to his energies and to the agent would be nearly impossible. There had to be someone who wouldn't be affected. Someone who could separate sex and love. Someone who could get him off without requiring the need for actual penetration.

"Abbi, could you turn around?" Simon groaned. He didn't want her staring at him, with a blank expression on her face. If anything, he wanted her to look upon him with eyes full of lust, longing and the knowledge that the very sight of her made him remember better times.

"Simon, are you ill? Your voice sounds strained." Abbi's image flickered slightly on the screen before him.

"I'm fine," he grunted. "Turn around, Abbi, *please*."

Abbi obeyed, as Bianca slid her hand down her smooth stomach.

Oh, that's it. Right there, baby, touch yourself right there. Just a little lower. Mmm, that's good.

Bianca responded to his mental push. Her hands obeyed his every desire as they glided over the shaven mound between her thighs. When she spread her legs, Simon caught a glimpse of her pink, wet pussy and increased the speed of his strokes. Bianca slid a finger over her clit and worked it in rapid circles. He wondered why she didn't just use one of the many pleasure toys the facility had available for seduction training.

She bucked her hips and used her free hand to squeeze her nipples. He could just imagine how good her ripe nipples would taste or how creamy her cunt was as she fingered it. When she bolted up on the bed and her legs went out straight, he knew she was coming. His balls tightened. He was about to come with her but at the very last minute he decided against it, wanting to conserve his energy.

Taking several deep breaths, Simon managed to calm his heart rate. In doing so, he slowed his body's need to ejaculate and was able to pinch the base of his cock hard enough to prevent it. This not only served to retain his power, which could temporarily become depleted during intercourse, but it also gave him added pleasure. For Simon, the act of sex wasn't about getting to the end in a hurry. It was about building and rebuilding pleasure.

Bringing her hand to her mouth, Bianca licked the cream from her wet fingertips and sent Simon's body into another state of need. His eyes rolled back in his head. He'd known from the first moment she'd be a wild one. The image of her licking the cream from each finger, savoring the taste of her own come was so incredibly erotic that he was sorry he'd only now decided to peek in on her. She'd soon be leaving Restigatio forever. It was hard to be sad when he knew she was off to meet her mate—the future father of her child.

"Do you wish to have audio, Simon?" Abbi faced him, not blinking once. The startling amount of deep blue in her eyes made him think of happier times. Quickly, he pushed the thoughts aside.

"No," Simon said, still fisting his hard cock. "No, audio won't be necessary. Please send for Bianca. Inform her that she's to meet me here in exactly three hours and that she is to come prepared to go on a mission. Don't give her the shots on this one."

All RLS agents were given shots to prevent against diseases and pregnancy on their regular missions. On their special missions, he didn't bother for they went to their future — their mates.

"A mission?" Abbi actually sounded surprised and that made Simon smile. She rarely got human emotions right.

"Yes, Abbi. A mission."

"Is Bianca ready for a mission? She's not completed every level of her agent training as of yet." A rundown of Bianca's personal file appeared on the screen.

Simon smiled. He knew enough to trust his powers and if they told him that the women would be paired with their future husbands soon, then he went with them — training completed or not. "She's completed enough. She will be safe where she's going and I have no doubt that she'll tame her charge with the greatest of ease."

"Tame her charge?" Abbi asked, the puzzlement in her voice evident.

"Program A-mac with the necessary files for the Kingdom of Vayre. Put a special emphasis on harem procedure and policy."

"A harem? But the assignimantor machine's last service check showed a virus. It is slight, yet still there. My censors are unable to indicate the effect it may have on file transfers."

Simon paused. "Hmm, does this virus pose any risk to the girls?"

"Negative. It is merely a glitch in the file transfer time."

"Run several more scans just to be sure. I won't have the girls harmed. If your data comes back the same, prepare the A-mac for mission launch. Delayed data transfer is a minimal risk."

"You are not concerned with the possible transfer problem?"

Simon sighed, not really wanting to continue to explain himself to a computer, but it was his own fault. He'd programmed Abbi for individual thoughts. Now he had no choice but to deal with her. "None of the agents leaving today will be harmed. Today is a special moment for us, Abbi. Today is the day we've waited for. It is the beginning of a new start for us all."

"Are the agents going to meet their mates?"

"Yes, but you are not to speak of it in front of them or any other RLS-69s."

Abbi nodded. "Yes, Simon. You have programmed me to speak of this with no one other than you or your associates. Unless directly ordered by you to disclose records."

"Correct."

"May I ask you something?"

Licking his hand again, Simon eased it back over his cock, enjoying the entire idea of voyeurism. Why hadn't he thought of this before? Of course the women sought self-pleasure. They talked about sex all day in training. He'd been blind not to realize it before. Although, to be fair, he had been extremely busy as well. "Mmm-hmm?"

"What will come of Bianca? Will she ever visit us again?"

Simon forced a smile on his face. "No, Abbi. Bianca will not return to us. She will marry and have a family."

"Can we visit her?"

"You can't travel, Abbi."

"Yes, but...but...Bianca's life-force will leave my sensor radius and I have grown accustomed to checking on her..."

"What you're trying to say is that you'll miss her." The very fact that Abbi had expressed any concern for Bianca was a good sign. However, as much as Simon wanted to explore the computer's ever-expanding abilities, he needed to relieve his hard-on and soon.

"Abbi, show me agent Sonja."

"Is she one of the agents going today as well?"

"Yes."

"My sensors have grown… I will miss her as well."

"Me too."

An image of a buxom redhead exiting the sparring room appeared on the screen in place of Bianca. Sonja walked down the long corridor to the locker room. The heavy door slammed shut behind her.

Simon grinned. It was impeccable timing. She'd be heading toward the showers.

He watched as Sonja removed her clothing piece by piece, nearing the showers as she undressed. Freeing her breasts, she let her fingers trail over them briefly before sliding her pants off. Simon squeezed his cock tighter when he saw that she wore no panties. He had no idea she was such a naughty girl.

The sweet curves of her hips left Simon thinking of how they'd feel as he held them tight, thrusting in and out of her body as he took her on her knees. When Sonja entered the shower, Abbi adjusted the viewing angle, giving him a wonderful shot of her lush body. He watched in silence, grasping his shaft as water pelted her flesh. When she moved and began to pleasure herself once more, tweaking her nipples and sliding her hand down her smooth stomach, Simon decided to bring her even more joy. It seemed only fair since he was gaining from the experience.

"Abbi, increase the shower temperature by several degrees and release the pheromone *acuerlfacere*."

"Simon, *acuerlfacere* is used to enhance a person's orgasm."

"She's earned it." Simon cast the screen a guarded look as Abbi nodded. She understood to follow his orders. "Also lock the locker room door and mark it as being cleaned so she won't be disturbed."

"Yes, Simon."

When Sonja's nipples noticeably hardened, he knew that the *acuerlfacere* was working. Her fingers went from functional to pleasuring. She stopped washing her body and began to knead her breasts. She lifted one and lowered her mouth. He pumped his cock feverously as Sonja managed to get her large breast up high enough to suck on her own nipple.

"That's it, baby. Suck it," he whispered.

"Excuse me, Simon, but I am unsure how to follow that order. Would you like me to start the protocols for issuing new commands into my — ?"

"Abbi," Simon shook his head, upset with the interruption. "Do not disturb me again unless it is an emergency."

He focused on Sonja again. She'd released her nipple from her mouth and left the shower. Disappointment flooded through Simon. The view of the locker room changed and he saw agent Sonja, soaked and staring at her image in the mirror. She moved closer to the mirror and licked her lips. Suddenly, she began to rotate her hips wildly. Leaning forward, Simon noticed that she had straddled the edge of the rounded sink counter and was using it to rub her clit. He'd never seen a woman so resourceful before and couldn't stop the burning in his loins.

Sonja rubbed herself against the counter harder, faster. As she looked into the mirror, Simon noticed her flushed cheeks.

"Rub harder, Sonja. Oh yeah, just like that. Pleasure yourself so I can see. That's it, sweetheart. Oh, fuck yeah. You like that don't you, baby? Rub harder, baby. I want to come watching you."

As if on demand, Sonja's body tightened. She rocked on the counter and he knew she was coming. He pumped his cock like a madman. Stroking it, pulling it, leaning back, readying himself for culmination. He was so close. So ready to come as he watched Sonja continue to rack every ounce of pleasure she could from the countertop.

"Ahh," he panted as his sac tightened. He was so close.

"Simon."

"Not…ahh…not now, Abbi."

"Simon."

"Abbi, I told you…"

The screen flickered and the image of Sonja rubbing the counter was immediately replaced by an image of Trinity, one of the first agents he'd ever selected. Simon slid down in his chair slightly, praying the edge of his desk concealed the fact that he had been jerking off. His body trembled violently, protesting the fact that it was so painfully close to coming.

He was about to pull his hand away from his still-hard cock but stopped when he looked into Trinity's face. She'd been with him a long time and was not only a trusted agent but a friend. The only reason he had decided against calling her image up on the screen was that she was one of the rare finds—a female who not only carried a large amount of human DNA in her but who also was well aware of it.

Simon released his cock and did his best to tuck it into his slacks so she didn't notice. He cleared his throat. "What's the problem, Trinity?"

"The problem is that you stuck me with the how to seduce a man course while Britney is on assignment. Why the hell couldn't Sasha do it? We all know she's a tramp. I'm wigging out here and you're sitting there with a smug look on your face."

Biting his lip, Simon did his best not to laugh. "Wigging out? Hmm, I take it that Abbi is still holding her midnight crash course vigils on the finer points of old Earth ways, slang and life. How in the universe she managed to get her database on a set of black market tutorials is beyond me."

"Yes, she is holding the vigils and we love it so leave her alone or I'll show you what going off on someone means."

"Trinity," Simon playfully scolded, all the while concentrating on how sexy she looked when she was angry. "You were saying?"

She rolled her blue eyes and flicked a piece of stray dark brown hair from her face. "Sasha's a tramp. Do you know that I caught her fucking another one of the prison guards last week?" Trinity tossed her hands in the air, not waiting for his response. Not that he would have dared to interrupt her while she was on a roll. Amused, Simon listened to her. "But Sasha being a tramp isn't why I need you down here. These pathetic excuses for male models you got us just came in and there is no way I can teach the girls how to do a thing with them."

Simon smiled. "You are more than qualified to instruct them on the finer points of making a man horny. I can attest to that." The minute he said it, he wanted to take it back. Trinity was to wed a close friend of his — another *figiutatio* — and it was wrong to imply that he wanted more from her even it was true.

Trinity moved a bit and he caught sight of her crowded classroom. Feeling guilty for having forced Trinity to assume responsibility for a course she obviously hated, he agreed to meet her.

Trinity was a special case. She was one of the few agents whose actual crime warranted them being here. She'd killed her uncle. Though, if she wouldn't have, Simon would've done it himself. The scoundrel had tried to pimp her out as a treat for his armies when she wasn't even of age yet. He'd also sold her two sisters into slavery. The very thought of two half-blooded human women being disposed of made his blood boil. For the others, like Bianca's intended mate, the little bit of DNA she carried didn't matter. But the less DNA the females carried, the less likely they'd be able to conceive a child with a *figiutatio*. Trinity was a rare find for his people. She was also pure of heart and that spoke volumes for her.

Simon stood and stared at the screen. Abbi's image reappeared. "Why didn't you warn me that Trinity was ringing through?"

"Simon, I made several attempts to notify you that a call was being issued but you silenced me."

Abbi had a point. He had been too focused on finding his first release in months to stop and listen to Abbi. "My apologies, Abbi. I'm just distracted right now."

Chapter Two

Simon entered the seduction training corridor and did his best not to laugh at the equipment hung along the walls. Whips, floggers, chains, cock rings — you name it, the RLS-69s had it at their disposal. He insisted that all the agents be trained not only in various forms of martial arts and weaponry but also in all the techniques needed to entice a man. He liked to think it was his helpful contribution to future husbands. If it just happened to make some of the girls more confident in their sexuality, then all the better.

His gaze filtered over to the section of sex toys that consisted of harnesses and bondage kits. His hard-on returned with a vengeance. Being tied up had never really been his thing but he had to admit that having a beautiful woman strapped to the bed did do something for him. Eyeing the cock harness, Simon arched an eyebrow, trying to imagine the various ways a toy of such a nature could be used.

Thank the gods he'd insisted on bringing in pre-made instructional videos when the RLS-69 program first launched. The idea of explaining, or in his case, attempting to show his first batch of agents how to use the endless collection of kinky toys didn't sit well with him. While he had found pleasure watching two of them masturbate today, he'd never actually touched one, yet. And most of the toys required a *lot* of touching.

Simon's cock jerked again. He took a deep, cleansing breath. It didn't help.

Thankfully, he'd never had to actually instruct the course. After the first batch of agents successfully completed the mission, they came to him and asked that the courses be taught by high-ranking agents from there on in—something about the computer and tapes not being entirely accurate. He didn't argue. Simon simply let the women decide amongst themselves who would teach what course and why. He did continue to teach other courses, involving weapons, self-defense and so on. But even those he would hand over to some of the more responsible senior agents most of the time.

While Trinity had mastered the art of seduction, she'd never been comfortable with the idea of using the skills on strange men. Knowing her background, Simon couldn't find it in himself to force her, or any of his girls for that matter, to use their sexuality as weapons. The choice was always theirs to make. He almost preferred they not have sex on missions unless it was with their chosen mate. He'd instituted a "seduce but don't fuck" policy early on and most of the girls abided by it.

Stopping near the entrance of Seduction Training Room Three, Simon laughed slightly when he noticed the button-operated moving mouth. It simulated fellatio and even had temperature control. Its humming action was well-renowned throughout the universe. Although he'd never actually tried one out, he had considered it. If the need to masturbate continued, he'd come back and grab one. No need to fly solo when a perfectly fuckable mouth was at his disposal.

Picking it up, he toyed with it. The object sprung to life as Simon inserted a finger into its gaping mouth. Much to his surprise, it felt very similar to the real thing. He shifted his weight uncomfortably. It felt really good.

The main reasoning for the wide collection of toys was that all of the Red Light Specialists had mates somewhere in the universe. Having the agents trained in the art of sex and seduction gave them the skills they'd need when dealing with many of the figureheads they'd be paired with. The skills also came in handy in tight pinches. Being male himself, he had to admit that it was easy to get distracted when a beautiful woman held his attention. The same rang true for the males of the universe. If the girls ran into trouble with an outside party, they could distract the man long enough to destroy him.

Some of his agents did actual missions, not just mating endeavors. The RLS-69s were called in when situations warranted the expertise of highly trained hired guns. The girls were more than qualified—each and every one of them. The ones that did actual missions had all completed their RLS training. They were well versed in hand-to-hand combat, weaponry and survival. They were their own brand of fighting machines. Ones that looked good in lingerie while they took out the bad guys.

Only a select few would go on multiple missions prior to being sent to their mate. Even then, they'd assume it was an actual mission from the word go. Because sometimes the fates made mistakes and even Simon was known to make a few. If he sent a specialist off with the knowledge they were to marry a man from their mission and something was to go wrong, she would be left to live life knowing that she'd missed out on her one true soul mate. And that, in his opinion, was the cruelest thing that could ever happen. Life experience had assured him he was correct.

"Uhh, are you coming in here to deal with the problem or are you planning on sliding that thing over your cock and having a go at it?"

Trinity's voice jerked Simon back to reality. Glancing down, he found that he had the mouth sucking on his finger. Embarrassed, he moved to put it back. He knocked one of the dildo harnesses off the wall and caught it with his other hand. Instantly, he found himself in a tangled mess of moving mouths and leather straps. Not prone to clumsiness, Simon groaned. Trinity's laughter only made matters worse. His already ragingly hard cock should have wilted out of mortification. It didn't. It homed in on the sultry sound of Trinity's naturally sexual voice and began to throb.

She was someone he considered a friend but that didn't change the fact that he also found himself attracted to her sexually. It stemmed from the fact that she carried a great deal of human DNA in her. That in itself called to him on a primal level. Add in the fact that she was not only drop dead gorgeous, she was a feisty fighting machine and Simon stood little chance in the "turn a blind eye" category.

Trinity reached out and grabbed hold of the harness, pulling him free of it. The look on her face said it all, but apparently she had more to offer. "Okay, if you're done with the one-man sex show, I'd like you to come in here and take a look at what you're making me work with."

Simon nodded, happy to have the change of subject. "Lead the way."

Trinity kept the harness in her hand and pushed the classroom door open. Several pairs of eyes turned to him. It was a relaxed atmosphere. Most of the girls sat on the floor, lounging against long pillows. There were a few comfortable chairs that were used a lot in demonstrations. All but a few wore tight pants, even tighter tank tops or cut-off shirts and boots.

Gillian, the newest recruit to date and by far the most innocent, looked wide eyed at the obscenely large rubber cock that hung from the harness.

Gillian wildly shook her head of silky blonde hair. "Oh no! I'm not putting that in me. Masturbation isn't right. I've already told you that I'd rather go back into the prison population than touch myself. I…"

"Would you please shut up," Trinity barked as she tossed the harness at Gillian, who acted as though a nuclear bomb had just been punted to her. "Play with it tonight. It might actually loosen you up."

"Or at the very least, get the stick out of her ass," Dahlia, a fiery redheaded agent, offered from the back of the room. Gillian looked like she was about to cry at the attack, her lips trembling. Simon cast Dahlia a wary glance and she shrugged her tiny shoulders. "Was it something I said?"

Gillian made a run for the door. It was evident by the hard look on Trinity's face and the rather large growl she let out that she was beyond annoyed with the girl. It was never a good thing when Trinity was upset, especially for the person she was upset with. Quickly, Simon grabbed Trinity's arm, not wanting her to give in and snap the girl's neck. It wasn't like her. Trinity was known for her physical restraint. It was usually her sharp tongue that did the most damage. Gillian must have pushed her way past her breaking point. "Abbi, lock the room, please."

"Yes, Simon," Abbi's voice came instantly from the computer console at the head of the class.

Trinity's eyes narrowed on Gillian. "You better get over your aversion to…"

Simon cut Trinity off quickly by taking a tighter hold on her arm. Gillian's destiny was already mapped out. Though, to be honest, Simon was nervous about that one. The naive woman was half human, didn't realize it, and destined for one of the most wildly sexual *figiutatio* he could think of. He'd been watching her for a while now and he didn't need Trinity frightening the poor woman more than she already was.

"What exactly did you call me down here for, Trinity?" he asked.

Her gaze locked on his and for a minute Simon wondered if Trinity would argue with him. It would be so very like her. She enjoyed pushing his limits more than most. Letting go of her arm, Simon watched as she pulled it slowly back. She would make a fine wife for his friend, who would no doubt require a woman willing to stand up to him.

"Fine. How the hell am I supposed to teach them to seduce a man with that?" She pointed to a life-sized mannequin in a chair in the corner of the room.

Simon wasn't sure how he'd missed it. He was about to ask what the problem was when he saw the dummy's penis, or lack thereof. Where there should have been a large ten-inch cock that went from flaccid to fully erect at the same speed a normal man would, there was an inch-high nub. Running his hand through his disheveled hair, he sighed. "They told me those were top of the line."

"Yeah," Trinity mused. "A very *short* line."

"Trin."

"Fine, I'll stop being a smart ass but seriously, Simon, what the hell am I supposed to do with that?"

"I'll put a call into the company tomorrow, love. I promise." He mentally scolded himself for slipping into old world habits. Lucky for him, many other planets had accents that sounded similar to his British one, though none were exact. And with the need to blend in so terribly important, Simon had to make a conscious effort to control what seemed so natural to him.

"Can we go now? It's not like that pathetic excuse for a dick is going to get any of us off," Bobbie, as she liked to be called, asked from behind Dahlia. She hid under a hat that reminded him so much of a baseball cap that he wondered where she'd gotten it from. She was an odd one, always wearing clothing so baggy that it was almost impossible to tell if she was male or female. Had he not seen her long brown hair upon her arrival on Restigatio, and her shapely figure during a sparring match, he wouldn't have been sure himself. Well, that and the visions he had of her mating and with child also helped.

"Thank you, Roberta…err…Bobbie, but training is vital and mastering the art of seduction can mean the difference between life and death." Simon looked to Trinity for backup. She merely shot him a bored expression and glanced toward the dummy.

"I vote we just beat the perp to a bloody pulp and be done with it. All in favor?" Bobbie asked, glancing around the room.

Dahlia, Bobbie, Trinity and a handful of other girls raised their hands. Simon's eyes almost popped out of his head when he noted that Abbi had her hand raised on the visual screen as well.

"Mutiny," Simon whispered, laughing to himself. He put his hands up and immediately the girls fell silent. "No, class is not dismissed. And the perp, as Abbi no doubt taught you, will remain unharmed. He can hardly be held accountable for what his maker forgot to hand out. Trinity is very resourceful. I'm sure she'll think of some way to instruct you all," he cleared his throat, "umm, without the aid of the mannequins."

Trinity huffed and then giggled. That was never a good sign. "Yep, I'm very resourceful. Simon, have a seat. You just won yourself a guest spot on how to seduce a man the RLS way."

Simon shook his head and took a step back. His cock was still in a state of ready and he knew better than to subject himself to the likes of these women. Once trained, his girls were like piranhas. If any one of the new girls attempted to order him around and demand he participate in something, he'd have given them a hard look and a stern talking to. Not much above that had ever been needed. They were good women whose crimes were laughable at times. Since it was Trinity, one of the few agents he considered a true friend, he went easy on her. "No. I'd rather not."

Trinity rolled her eyes. It was a move that only a handful of his girls would dare to do in his presence. The girls respected him as their director and never counteracted an order when it was important. Even though they were technically prisoners, they weren't treated as such once they joined RLS training. Simon knew that he had to show them trust if they were to trust him. For that reason, they were given leave to go about the facility as they wished. Besides, he'd have to trust them when they went out on missions. If he treated them like children, then he could expect them to act like children. If he treated them like adults with minds, they wouldn't let him down. He was sure of it.

Simon knew what he was doing when he picked them and knew that they could be trusted to keep their word of honor. They might have made a few mistakes, but when it came down to it they were honorable, loyal women. Besides, it wasn't like they could escape the RLS facility unless he wanted them to.

"Yeah," Trinity said. "I'd rather not be instructing this course when I'm supposed to be teaching self-defense, so we're even. Now, have a seat."

Against his better judgment, Simon sat in the chair. Trinity grabbed his suit jacket and removed it quickly. Feeling his cock stir at the idea of finally getting contact other than his hand, he came to his senses and attempted to stand up. She caught hold of his shirt collar and planted her body firmly between his now-spread legs. The tiny white tank top she wore left her dark nipples showing through. It would be his luck that this would be one of Trinity's braless days.

"You did remember that you're leaving on a mission later today, didn't you?" he asked, directing his gaze to her see-through top.

Abbi gasped. "Agent Trinity is to leave on a mission today as well?" The shocked look in her eyes told Simon why she asked. She knew that the women leaving today most likely wouldn't be back if their matings were successful. Abbi bowed her head. "Excuse me for a moment, there is an electrical disturbance in my sensory unit."

Simon's heart ached for her. Abbi would miss Trinity, as would he, but it was for the best.

Trinity smiled down at him. "Like I could forget that I had a mission. And it doesn't really matter if I show up wearing a clown costume or naked, Abbi and the A-mac machine dress us accordingly each and every time."

Okay, she had him there. He would have thought of that himself but stroking his cock to the very erotic, very naked scenes that Bianca and Sonja had shown left him so horny that his resolve, and his thought processes, were weak. Sitting with Trinity's ample breasts thrust into his face only made them crumble more. He licked his lips and leaned back.

Trinity pushed her knee between his thighs, nudging his groin in the process and pressed her chest into his face. "Okay, ladies. This, while great for grabbing their attention, hardly works in the real worlds. Unless of course, he's a complete slimeball, then titty fuck away!" She laughed at her own joke and continued on, "I'd suggest something more on the line of this…"

She flicked her tongue out and over his neck, stopping only when she came to his ear. Blowing softly, she caused the hair on the back of his neck to stand on end. Simon squirmed. His cock now hard enough to lift his slacks high off his waist.

"Ahh…umm…I'm sure they get the idea now." Scanning the room, he grabbed the only thing in reach—a red handbag. He thrust it into his lap to hide his erection. Sheepishly, he looked down and then up at Trinity. "Just wondering what Abbi sends with you ladies."

"Mmm-hmm." Trinity bent close to him again and did a soft laugh technique that sent shivers down his spine. Splaying her hands through the back of his hair, she pulled his head toward her. "If you move the man's head up so he can see your face, you need to make him feel like he's all you're thinking of. If you're not a good actor then launch directly into kissing or nibbling on the bottom lip. Tease his mouth. The longer you play with it, the closer you get him to ejaculating. Get him to do that during this seduction phase and you stand a good chance of not having to follow through with intercourse."

"Excuse me," Dahlia asked, raising her hand. "But what if we want to have sex with them?"

Trinity grit her teeth and Simon feared she'd not only verbally lash out at Dahlia but physically as well. Her nerves weren't what they usually were. He brought his power up quickly and concentrated on concealing it from the girls. It ran through his body and danced over Trinity's smooth skin. Instantly, her gaze snapped to his. Before he could stop her, she was straddling his waist and biting at his neck, mouth, jaw, anything she could get her mouth on. She swayed her hips and rubbed her pussy against the handbag on his lap. Its contents dug into his crotch and he was sure that a ball would be impaled at any minute.

Simon could have used his power to thrust Trinity away from him, but doing that would cause her pain and he would never harm one of his girls. He tried another approach. He attempted to move her by lifting her. All *figiutatio* possessed inhuman strength but as Trinity ripped the handbag out from between them, the very last of his resolve faded away.

Wildly, she rubbed her body against his, dry humping him with more passion than he'd seen in a long while. Already hard from earlier endeavors, Simon heard Trinity draw in a deep breath as her cunt pressed madly against him.

Quickly, he tried to pull his magic back. He'd forgotten how susceptible full-blooded humans were to it. Being that Trinity was half human, she was prone to respond to his power.

Trinity bit his lower lip and sucked hard on it. She growled. Simon jerked beneath her, fighting to keep her from unfastening his slacks and himself from ripping her shirt off. When Trinity's body tightened against him and her breathing all but stopped, Simon knew she was coming. The need for release had been upon him for hours and having a beautiful woman cresting against his still-clothed penis was more than he could handle. His cock pulsated as semen shot out of it, filling the insides of his underwear. Trinity continued to rub against him, causing his come to soak through the front of his slacks.

Hitting his zenith caused his powers to fade away quickly. They ripped back fast, leaving not only him but Trinity as well. She slumped forward and he caught her around the waist. Simon's body was tired, spent and sated. He patted Trinity's back and almost laughed at the fact they'd both just found release by dry fucking and yet he still gave her a chaste pat.

"Wow, and here I thought we wouldn't learn anything today," Dahlia murmured in a hushed tone.

Simon froze and Trinity bolted off him. Her wide blue eyes looked puzzled then pissed. She narrowed her gaze on him and then lowered it. An odd, sadistic smile played across her lips and Simon glanced down. To his horror, his gray slacks looked as though he'd wet them. In many ways he had. Quickly, he dove for the red handbag and covered himself. The other agents didn't seem to notice yet and without his powers, he had no way of creating the illusion of the semen not being there. Only Trinity had seen and only she knew what he'd just done.

Embarrassed by his lack of control, Simon stood slowly. He kept the handbag tucked tight to his body and made his way to the door. "Well, ladies, I think Trinity did a wonderful job considering the circumstances." He cleared his throat and chanced a look at Trinity.

"But I was going to see if there was anyone who wanted to practice," Trinity began, smiling too innocently.

"No. Sorry. I have lots of work to do." Simon nodded at the group. A little flustered, he added, "Thanks for your hard work."

The smile was still on Trinity's lips but now she'd added an odd arch of her dark eyebrows to it, making her look like the vixen she was. "Oh, no, thank you, Simon. I think everyone got one hell of a lesson. And thanks for sitting in for Recessive Stubby over there." She pointed back at the mannequin but kept her eyes on him.

He shifted awkwardly. "Right then, class dismissed. Abbi, unlock the door."

"Yes, Simon, and I am detecting a new emission in the training wing. Shall I run a scan on it?"

"A new emission?" Simon asked.

"Yes, Simon. It appears to be a fluid of some…"

Fluid?

It hit him then what Abbi was sensing—his semen. "No, Abbi! Umm, no scan is necessary. Thank you."

The agents filed out of the room, one after another, until all twenty of them were gone. Trinity strolled over to him and reached for his groin. He jerked back. "Relax," she said with a smile. "I just want the damn handbag back. It's part of the training and if you take off with it then Britney is screwed when she gets back. You wouldn't want anyone to be *screwed,* would you, Simon?"

"Do you have something you'd like to say, Trin?"

"Nope." She winked. Glancing down she laughed. "Uhh, but you might want to change before you meet with the departing agents today."

* * * * *

"Agents Bianca, Sonja and Trinity, please enter the assignimantor machine's transfer pods," Abbi said.

Simon watched Abbi's carefully guarded expression and felt a bit bad for giving her the ability to free think. He'd once hoped she'd learn human emotions, but as he watched her struggling to understand the conflict within her sensors, he had second thoughts.

"Where are we going?" Bianca asked as she climbed into the long, sleek orange tube. "No place with stone, right?"

"He won't tell you. I heard he never tells anyone," Sonja answered. She cast a wary look at Simon, as if she'd forgotten he was in the room, and then climbed into her pod. "I just hope it's somewhere that doesn't have bugs. I found another *gelipson* bug in my quarters today. You guys should really do something about those."

Abbi sniffed and nodded. "I will."

Sonja gave the image a strange look and Abbi put on a brave face.

Simon didn't bother commenting. Sonja was right. He never told any of the agents about their missions. The A-mac did a perfectly fine job of handling the information they needed. Each agent would be supplied with the data required to exist on the foreign planet and detailed descriptions of their objective. While the virus in the A-mac was unfortunate, Abbi had assured him that the agents were in no danger, so he'd okayed the departure.

His associates were even watching in on this mission launch. Simon's power had been spent after his orgasm and he had to wait for it to charge up before he'd been able to project the image of the room out to the associates. They were observing from the safety of their main headquarters on screens much like the one he'd used to watch the girls masturbating. Cameras were not permitted in the A-mac room or in Simon's office. None would dare go against his request so he didn't fear they'd spy on him. He was powerful, a force that even the other council members feared and admired.

Trinity moved up behind him and tapped his shoulder. She winked at him and went to climb into her pod. He caught her arm and gave her a warm smile. "Goodbye."

Her brow furrowed. "Simon? Are you okay?"

"Fine. Why?"

"Uhh, you never say goodbye."

"Well, today I do." He looked at the departing agents. "Take care of yourselves and have safe journeys."

They glanced at each other nervously. He wanted to ease their fears but couldn't reveal the details of what he hoped would occur. Trinity's gaze fell upon him and he could see the hesitation in her face. He knew he'd been the first person she'd trusted since her parents died and seeing her doubt him hurt. "I'll speak with you soon. Now, prepare for departure."

Trinity obeyed his command as all his agents did. He waited as Abbi activated the A-mac. The light buzz in the room signified it was working. The girls closed their eyes and prepared to transfer. As they began to fade, Simon waved to them all.

"Go to your futures, ladies," he whispered.

They vanished and he stopped projecting the image of them to the council. Then he turned to walk out. The door to the room slammed shut and he looked back at the screen. "Abbi?"

"How many more of the agents will leave to find mates?"

He sighed. "All of them. Not right away, of course, but at some point they all will have mates. If our plan works, we'll continue to find new women with matching DNA traits and pair them up as well."

"I see."

"Abbi, what's wrong?" Simon studied the image of her.

"Will I be sent away too?"

Simon laughed softly. "No, Abbi. You will never be sent away."

"Will you leave me, Simon? Will you go on a mission and never return?"

Simon went to say no, but stopped. "Perhaps, but I have not foreseen such a thing."

Part Two
Bianca

Chapter One

Bianca's body was tossed into a wall. For a moment, she stood pressed to the hard surface, stunned that the damned A-mac had actually spit her out onto stone. If she wanted stone, she could've stayed on Restigatio, where she'd spent four years in the mines. If not for Director Simon's offer of rehabilitation, she'd still be there—sleeping in some dark hole in between digging shifts, her hands bleeding and raw, her body always aching.

Rehabilitation.

Bianca snorted. What a fool she'd been when she signed on for that. She actually thought she would spend a few months saying she was sorry to a counselor in a halfway house, repenting her sins and begging forgiveness for her heinous crimes.

Instead, she was sent to a training facility where they taught her how to fight and, more importantly, how to seduce. They turned her into a Red Light Specialist, part of the RLS-69s. She was elite now, special.

She was *especially* annoyed to have landed on stone.

"I specifically said no stone. Was it really too much to ask?" Agent Bianca rolled her eyes. Gingerly, she pushed away from the hard barrier and grumbled, "Ouch."

Bianca took a deep breath, trying to get her bearings. Big, evenly cut blocks of gray stone lined the walls of a long hallway. Torches lit the otherwise dim area. It wasn't much to go on.

This is an alien planet? Looks more like the images of those Medieval Earth castles Abbi showed us. Blessed Stars! I'm not in a place that primitive, am I? Damn it, Simon! I thought those images were just so we could make fun of old Earth culture, not an actual training lesson.

"This blows!" Bianca frowned.

Her mission was supposed to have downloaded into her brain during the transfer to the planet. Maybe it wouldn't be as bad as she first feared. Concentrating, she had no clue what she was doing or where she was. Although, she was thinking in a different language, so that was something at least. It meant the information she'd been embedded with was working. Now, if only she could find a place to hide for an hour or so while her brain released the rest of her assignment.

The A-mac embedded everything she needed into her head during transfer. But Abbi had warned her that the brain could only take in so much at once and sometimes, due to the sudden burst of new information, it had to recharge afterward. That would account for half of the headache she now had. The damned stone wall would account for the other half.

Bianca decided to find a good hiding spot until she knew what she was up against. Feeling a chill against her legs as she began to walk, she glanced down and caught sight of what the A-mac had dressed her in. She froze, unable to make her feet move.

"Ah, blazes, no!" she swore. "Come on, guys! You have got to be kidding me! Ha! Ha! Ha! Rookie hazing joke is now over. Get me out of here."

Bianca waited, hoping she'd be jerked back to the training facility. Nothing changed. Damn! She'd really hoped this one was a joke. She was going to strangle Simon and Abbi when she saw them next. Then she'd strangle the A-mac.

This was just too humiliating. She could see every last stitch of skin through the thin red gauze of her nonexistent outfit. She might as well be naked. Well, to be fair, there was a triangle piece of cloth over the thin thatch of hair guarding her pussy and two more tinier triangles fitted over her nipples.

Grimacing, she tipped her head back, doing her best to see what the back half of her looked like. Yep. It too was covered only in the thin veil. Turning in a circle, she caught the slightest glint of light further down the hall. It was a long mirror. Going to check out her outfit, she posed before her reflection. Her eyes were lined with thick, black makeup and her cheeks had been painted a bright red with rouge. She didn't care for the makeup, but her body looked damned good in the outfit.

"Hmm, not bad," she said to herself. Good thing her ass was sexy and toned. She flexed it for effect, tensing, releasing, tensing, releasing, jiggling it fast to make the muscles ripple under the almost nonexistent weight of the red material. Not bad. Not bad at all. Four years of lifting boulders could really tone up a figure. It still didn't mean she wanted her ass out for the world to see, but hey, as long as she was the only one looking...

"This is a dance I have not seen before."

As the words rolled over her, Bianca shivered with feminine awareness. It was the first male voice, besides Simon and the prison guards, that she'd heard in nearly four years. It was deep, low, sexy...

Wait a minute. Whoever it belonged to was watching her wiggle her ass.

Blazes!

Think, think, think.

Bianca's first instinct was to beat up the guy. Well, the A-mac would surely give her the instincts she needed. Fighting it was!

Bianca focused on where the voice came from. Twirling on her heels, she threw out her fist. For a brief second, she saw incredibly dark eyes before focusing on a white mist. Her fist went through the mist and hit the stone wall.

"Ah, sacred comet!" she gasped, cradling her injured hand. She'd swung hard. Now her knuckles were bleeding and she couldn't move her fingers. So much for her dominant fighting hand.

"That looks like it hurt," the man's voice continued. He was behind her. He sounded amused, mocking. "I would not have done that, *gengli.*"

"Listen here," Bianca said, spinning around to face him. Her gaze fell on a dark face with features carved to perfection. Everything she'd been about to say to him was forgotten. How long had it been since she'd seen a handsome man that wasn't Simon? A half-naked, handsome man? Obviously too long, because she boldly let her gaze roll over his muscled chest. Fires sparked to life in her sex, drenching her pussy. If she wasn't on a mission, she would've thought nothing of thrusting this fine specimen up against the wall and demanding he fuck her brains out.

His skin was bronzed, marred only by a black tattoo running down the center of his chest to the navel carved into his rippled abdomen. A white linen loincloth fitted around his waist, higher in back, only to dip down low in front.

The loincloth was long, falling in pleats to his calves. It showed off his hipbones and a small tuft of hair leading in a trail down to the exposed top of his genitals, but the garment wasn't revealing enough to be overly indecent. Bianca was disappointed by this. By the way her body heated, and the way cream built between her thighs, it was clear four years was too long a time to go without a man. Sure, she'd pleasured herself, but it wasn't the same. Her finger in her passage felt nothing like a man's hard cock thrusting in, filling her up, making her come. There had been plenty of sex toys, but it still wasn't the same.

"I can see by the way you stare, you know who I am." The man almost seemed disappointed.

Bianca thought it best to play along. Absently, she answered, "Yes."

"Pity." His voice was soft, spine-tingling rich. "I was looking forward to what you would do next."

"Really?" Bianca smirked. She smiled before moving her bare foot out to kick him in the stomach. Hey, her instincts were still telling her she needed to beat the guy up. That, or sleep with him.

Her foot should've hit flesh, it instead fell through the white mist as the man disappeared. The mist filtered into her gauze pant leg, caressing against her skin as it worked its way up. She gasped, holding her leg out to the side. It was as if she could feel a thousand fingers caressing, many mouths licking and kissing her at the same time. The mist traveled up to her slick folds and massaged her clit.

"*Ahh!*" she gasped as blood rushed to the neglected little nub. She caught her flushed reflection in the mirror. Her kohl-lined eyes were wide. There was nowhere to run.

Jolts worked their heated way over her, making her nipples hard little pebbles. Whatever this mist man was, he was using his power to suck on her clit. She allowed her leg to fall back down from the kick. She needed it to support her weight before her whole body collapsed into an orgasmic heap.

Just as quickly as it went in, the mist moved down her other leg and filtered out. Breathing hard, and so very aroused now that she'd been caressed by a cloud, Bianca turned. The handsome man materialized before her, the mist solidifying. He licked his lips as his lids fell lazily over his dark eyes.

"You will do, *gengli*," he said. "Your taste is tempting and I do not detect my brothers to have claimed you. Meketre will be sorry he missed your taste."

Hey, why not invite him to join the party. If he looks anything like you we can make it a threesome.

It took Bianca a minute to collect her thoughts. When she did, she frowned. "Excuse me?"

"Meketre, my brother. He and the others just left," the man explained.

"No, I got that Meketre was your brother. I meant the other thing. I will do? My taste is tempting? That thing."

"I look for sexual release, *gengli*. You may come to my bedchamber to bring me pleasure." The man motioned his hand, turned his back on her and walked down the hall.

Bianca watched him and frowned. He didn't even look to see if she obeyed. It was like he assumed she'd just follow him because he was horny. When he turned the corner, she took off running in the other direction, careful to keep her footsteps light so he didn't hear her. It wouldn't do for the arrogant mist man to come back.

"I may come to give you pleasure, my ass!" she grumbled under her breath, running faster, needing to put as much distance as she could between the egotistical man and herself. Besides, she needed to find a place to hide until the planet's information was released from within her head. "I'll show you release, all right. I'll release you from your mortal coil, you arrogant son of a bitch!"

* * * * *

Prince Ahmet pushed open his bedchamber door. The chamber was richly decorated with the finest of silks and gauze in the kingdom. Pottery vases lined the wall, filled with native plants and fruit trees. Spiral designs decorated them. The vases were offerings from his people and decorated almost every room of his home. Not all of his people could afford great gifts, but that did not stop Ahmet from taking pleasure in them.

Those peasants who did not give vases gave a wealth of other tributes—necklaces of precious and semiprecious stones, small hand-carved statues depicting his people. The richer men of his kingdom prided themselves by giving fine tribute. The nobles gave large statues of bronze and gold, intricate carved furniture and great weaponry.

The bedchamber reflected the wealth and power of Ahmet's position as the eldest son and future king. Well, he'd be king already, except for the small fact he didn't find any woman worthy of being his queen. It didn't matter. As far as the Kingdom of Vayre was concerned, he was their ruler. The rest was just a title. Oh, and there was the small matter of the great power he'd receive with the title, but thus far he didn't need it.

Gold encrusted the posts of the bed — a bed so large it could hold ten people easily. Ahmet knew from experience, having taken nine women to his bed once. It had been a most pleasurable night. He'd rested on his back, doing hardly a thing as he watched the women pleasuring him. Their mouths sucked and kissed every inch of his flesh. Their sweet bodies had released the seed from his cock not only with their mouths but with their pussies and asses as well. They'd ridden him good, one after another, bathing him in warm water and rubbing him in oils between releases. As he was fucked, they also provided great entertainment, releasing each other while he watched. It had been a most glorious night, one he should repeat soon.

The taste of the strange harem woman was still on his lips. He was sure he would've remembered if he took her, though he'd taken many women to his bed and it was hard to tell one from another. Her taste was sweet, flowing in his blood. Because of this, he could even forgive the fact that she didn't curtsey to him in the hall. He stood, his back to the door, waiting for it to close, waiting for her to begin her seduction of him. A smug look settled over his features. The harem women knew that as future king he couldn't seduce them, but must be seduced. He was above them and it was their privilege to see to his pleasure.

Any second now, he thought, waiting for the caress of her hands, the kiss of her lips. His cock was hard, aching, ready to be massaged. If she pleased him, he'd allow her to stay the night so that she may bathe him and suck on him. It was a great privilege to drink royal seed.

Ahmet waited, his erection pressing up against the front of his loincloth, straining for that first feel of contact. Nothing came. The prince scowled. He was not one to put off his desires.

Slowly, turning on his leather sandals, he looked in disbelief at the empty doorway. Glancing around the bedchamber, he found it empty and went to look out into the hall. She wasn't there. The woman didn't follow him as he'd commanded her to do. His eyes narrowed. It angered him that he would be aroused with no one to ease the ache from his loins.

His power surged. Outside, it started to rain. It wasn't a good thing when he wasn't happy.

* * * * *

"Ah, sacred comet." Bianca stayed curled in the strange broom closet, hitting her head back against the stone in frustration. "Sacred comet, this is bad!"

She whispered her father's favorite curse over and over again. It was the only thing the man had really ever taught her that she found of use. When he died, he left everything to her brother. Bianca hadn't had a choice but to earn money anyway she could. It was either gambling or prostitution. Some days, she was convinced she should've tried her hand at prostitution. Maybe then she wouldn't be in this mess.

Her past mistakes weren't what made her so upset. It was the fact that more and more of her assignment was being released to her. It seemed the man she'd run off on was some sort of royal prince. At least, she was pretty sure that's what his black tattoo meant. Since there were twelve royal princes, it was hard to know which one Mr. Come Please Me was. She just hoped it wasn't the future king. Though odds were against it — it was a one in twelve chance that he was the man she was looking for.

Bianca was dressed as a harem girl, thus the see-through outfit. It would make sense. She pretty much felt like a cheap hooker. Oh, and it explained why the man had kept calling her *gengli* . According to her translation, it meant whore.

Lovely bunch of men, these royals.

Her mission was pretty straightforward. Women from the future king's harem were disappearing. It was suspected, but not proven, that they were being killed. There were no bodies, no leads, no known motives. It was Bianca's mission to discover where the girls were. Bianca's first instinct was that the prince himself killed the women. It would make explain why there was no evidence. All it would take is a simple order to the palace guards to have the matter covered up. He probably was some sick pervert into snuff.

Though the one kink in that logic was the king was the one who'd contacted RLS to check out the disappearances. It didn't mean the king wasn't a suspect. In fact, she wasn't supposed to tell him who she was and why she was there because he was one. He didn't even know she was coming or that the RLS-69s had taken the case.

There was another option. The prince could just be mad because his women were running away from him. If it happened right after sex, it stood to reason that the man was terrible in bed. Maybe the women were bored and went to hide out with the palace guards. Bianca couldn't say she blamed the women. According to her information, the prince wasn't allowed to seduce a woman and barely allowed to actively give her pleasure unless it pleased him to do so, which *never* happened. Details got a little fuzzy, but if he gave pleasure it indicated something important.

Yeah, like he had to actually work.

"Great," she said, her voice low and sarcastic. "Just what I always wanted, an unenthusiastic man that lies there like a cold fish while I do all the work. It's like a dream come true."

Because of the possible nature of the crimes, Bianca was going to get a firsthand go at Mr. Royal. It's not exactly the way Simon would suggest handling the case. He did have that "seduce but don't fuck" policy. Good thing policies were meant to be broken. Having sex with the king would be the fastest way to get this mission over with.

Could it be the king was killing the women to hide a shameful secret? Maybe he'd have a small cock and then the case would be closed. She really, really hoped he didn't have a small cock. It might make her assignment easier but wouldn't do a thing for the ache in her pussy. Why did that stupid mist guy have to caress her like that? Now all she could think about was how horny she was.

Bianca took a deep breath and tried to ignore the fact that her nipples were still hard with just the memory of the arrogant man's touch. She had to focus on the mission. Complete the mission and then she could get out of here.

She was supposed to get chosen by this future king, Hamet or Hammock or Ahmet—blazes, she wasn't clear on the name yet. Once chosen, she'd get the "honor" of fucking his brains out and then waiting around to see what happened next.

The door to the closet swung open. "I thought I heard someone in there. Get out! What do you think you're doing? Haven't you heard the call? All harem girls are to report to the harem. Prince Ahmet wishes to find a bed partner for the night."

"Ahmet?" She tried to see if that was the name she was looking for. Yep. Prince Ahmet, future king to the Kingdom of…uh, yeah, something. That's the man she was supposed to seduce. Looking at the woman, she asked, "And the harem would be where?"

"That's why you're hiding," the elderly woman said. As she stepped aside, Bianca saw that she had short white hair plastered to her head. She smelled like onions and it stood to reason the woman worked in the kitchen. "You're new. Well, it's not the first time this has happened. I'm going to give you some advice though. When you hear the bells, get to the harem. If the princes have you in mind and you're not there, they can get mighty angry. We all know what happens when royalty gets angry. Now, come on, I'll walk you to the harem this one time."

Bianca stood and was led down the long stone hall. "I'm Bianca."

"Magha," the woman answered.

"What happens when royalty gets angry?"

"What do you think happens? They're descendents of the gods. When they're displeased, everyone feels it. It's why you harem women are so important. It's the pleasures you provide that keep the royal princes from getting frustrated and temperamental. Why else do you think you're treated like queens?"

"So, what? They cut off people's heads when they get cranky?" Bianca frowned, making a mental note to try and not beat up the king like she did his brother. Stiffening, she thought of the prince in the hall. "You may come to give me pleasure, my ass! Jerk."

"What?"

"Oh, ah, nothing. You were saying?" Bianca forced a smile. Spending all that time alone in a mine shaft had given her some bad habits. She really needed to stop talking to herself.

"They haven't yet. It depends on which prince was upset. With Prince Ahmet, we could have floods. Actually, it's started to rain so he must be in a dour mood already. It's no wonder he called the harem. Anyway, with Prince Meketre there could be a plague of insects that destroys everything in their path—lice, flies, boils, sores. Prince Duat and Prince Khufu can cause hail, boiling rivers of blood, famine, endless days of darkness—"

"I get the point," Bianca rushed. "Keep the royal guys happy. Gotcha."

Magha led Bianca to a set of wide double doors. Pushing on them, she motioned Bianca to step inside. The harem was a long marble hall with lounge seats next to bathing pools. It smelled like lavender, rosemary and some sort of spice she wasn't familiar with. She saw burning pots of incense near the opposite wall.

The harem women were all humanoids and were dressed as indecently as Bianca. They lounged in a colorful array of gauze. Their eyes were darkened with thick, black makeup and their cheeks turned a bright red with rouge. Bianca grimaced, reminded of what her face looked like.

"Livena," Magha said. "This is Bianca. She's new, come to replace the others."

Livena was a tall woman, slender and willowy with large gray eyes that were nearly colorless. Her waist-length black hair was parted in the center of her forehead, the long bangs pulled to either side of her face. The color was a stark contrast to her snow white features. Bianca shivered, feeling very cold by the way the woman looked at her.

Livena rudely looked Bianca over and shook her head. "You are to bow to me. I am harem mistress."

Bianca sighed, bending at the waist. Her body moved automatically, sweeping her arms out to the side as she lowered her breasts toward the floor. The A-mac obviously gave her gestures as well.

Livena merely nodded in return. "You are new."

"I am," Bianca answered.

The woman frowned. "Only speak when asked a question."

"But, you just asked if I was new."

"No, I stated that you were new," Livena corrected.

"No, you—"

"Silence!" Livena bellowed. "For your insolence, I forbid you from being presented to the prince today and sentence you to twenty lashes."

Bianca paled.

"Guards!" Livena yelled. Suddenly, three very hunky men appeared dressed in black loincloths. They were all built, finely toned, lean of muscle. They all bowed their heads at Livena's order.

Bianca felt her skin tingle. There was something too familiar in the way the men looked at the harem mistress. They eyed her body as if they had intimate knowledge of it. Bianca hid her smile. She'd bet a thousand space credits that Livena had fucked the harem guards.

Oh, wait. She shouldn't bet anything. That's how she ended up here in the first place.

"Take this woman to be punished." Livena motioned at her. "Fifty lashes."

"Hey," Bianca said before she could stop herself. "You said twenty before."

"Seventy-five lashes." Livena curled her lips into a devious smile, daring Bianca to again talk out of turn.

"Wait a minute." Bianca lifted her hand in defense as the guards moved to grab her arm. She looked around for help. Magha was gone and the other harem women merely watched, quiet and unmoving. "I said hold on!"

"One hundred lashes!" Livena announced. The harem women gasped. Their gauze-covered bodies began to sway in a frenzy of movement and their murmurs rose over the marble hall.

"That is a harsh punishment for one so frail."

Bianca stopped struggling and the guards' hands bit into her flesh. Livena turned on her heels and immediately dropped to the floor, kneeling low in respect. The harem women did the same. Bianca had no intention of moving, but the guards roughly pushed her to her knees as they too kneeled. They let go of her arms.

Two sandaled feet stepped before her. She slowly looked up, moving her eyes over two very masculine calves. The calves molded into thighs that disappeared beneath a bothersome loincloth. Bianca frowned at the material, forgetting for a moment where she was as she let her eyes roam higher. The man stood with authority and she found it tremendously arousing. Seeing the black tattoo on the rippled stomach, she paused.

Oh no! It couldn't be…no. Bianca swallowed before looking all the way up. *Ah, hell! Yeah, it definitely is him. Mr. Royal is back. Shit. Shit.* "Shit."

"Shit?" the prince asked.

Fuck. Did she whisper that out loud? At least it wasn't in the prince's native language.

"What is this 'shit'?" he asked.

"Ah," Bianca glanced around, trying to see if anyone had heard what she said. People were looking at her, but none seemed to understand her word. It was one Abbi had taught her. "It's my native form of greeting, your...ah...Excellently Royal Highness, ah, sir."

"Shit," he said, nodding.

Bianca grinned. That was too close. "Mm-hmm."

"Livena?" the prince asked.

"Yes, Prince Ahmet," Livena straightened slightly.

Oh, great. Mr. Jerkoff was the future king? Great going, slick!

"What is her crime to warrant such a punishment?"

"Insolence, Your Highness." Livena turned to glare at her from her place on the floor.

"A dire thing indeed," Ahmet said. When he looked at her, his brow arched on his forehead, she had a feeling he might be thinking about her earlier "insolence" in the hallway. Oh, like when she tried to punch the future king!

Think, think, think. How do I get out of this one?

Bianca licked her lips. Instantly, her mind told her to seduce the future king. Her hands tingled with the consuming desire to touch him. She looked at them, wondering at the sensation. Then, deciding the urge was put there by the A-mac, she went with it.

Bianca crawled forward, closing the short distance between them. She was very aware that she was about to publicly grovel and didn't like it one bit. Well, okay, maybe she liked it just a teeny tiny bit. But she really didn't have a choice either way. She'd insulted the future king once by refusing to pleasure him, unintentionally jeopardizing her mission. She thought of the mines. There was no way she was going back there. And more immediate was the threat of being lashed a hundred times. Like it or not, she had to play the part of the submissive and seduce Prince Ahmet.

Bianca touched his calves. She felt him stiffen beneath her palms. His flesh was warm, almost hot. Cream dripped out of her. She bit her lip, trying her best not to think of how little the gauze material protected her from everyone's view. Already she could feel it sticking between her thighs, attesting to her great arousal.

Bianca gripped his legs, just feeling his flesh for a moment. Blazes, it had been so long since she'd felt warm male skin. A tingling began in her nipples, working primal lust throughout her entire body. Her pussy clenched, wanting to be filled to the brim with hard cock.

Before she realized what she was doing, she was rubbing up his legs, inching forward until her hands could slide up his thighs beneath the loincloth. Her mouth watered. She wanted to taste him, take his cock into her mouth. The material rose before her face, stirring as he became aroused by her actions.

She smiled. Size was definitely not the issue with this man. He was more than well enough endowed to please any woman. Bianca just hoped her cunt wasn't so tight from lack of use that he'd hurt her when he pried her apart with it. Just the thought actually made her clit pulse.

Bianca forgot the eyes of the harem watched her. She forgot everything but the sting of her wet pussy, the throbbing of her clit, the need to be fucked. Pushing her hands higher, she explored around the sides of his thighs, feeling around to his ass. To her pleasure, she found him naked beneath the loincloth.

It was too much. She needed to be touched. His hands didn't move from his sides, even as she silently willed them to. Leaning in, she breathed deeply, taking in the intimate smell of his sex.

Bianca wasn't sure how it happened, but she actually felt more cream building, making her so slick that each movement of her hips was like a deep caress. Her eyes flickered upward, meeting his dark, piercing gaze. She wanted more, but something made her pause.

Permission. She was waiting for his permission. The realization stunned her and she fought the urge to obey him. Bianca had never been one to wait for a man's permission. The need was too great. Her hands trembled and she could feel her mind close to breaking the invisible barrier the A-mac created that kept her back.

Blasted A-mac!

Chapter Two

Ahmet watched the woman before him, completely stunned at her daring. Yet he couldn't bring himself to stop her as she touched him. She stayed on her knees before him. Cool hands ran over his ass, squeezing, prying his cheeks apart slightly as she kneaded them, giving him a hint that she would do more as her fingers slipped intimately close to delving into his cleft.

Her breasts rose and fell beneath the thin red gauze of her clothing and he smelled the heady fragrance between her thighs. He just knew her cream was preparing her cunt for his enjoyment. She was ready, in heat. She wanted to be fucked. Just knowing she wanted him as badly as he wanted her did something to him.

His cock rose, thick and strong. He wanted to thrust it between her lush parted lips, fucking her enchanting mouth. Feeling the eyes of the harem on him, he glanced around. Everyone was staring. He didn't care and was pleased that the woman before him was so bold as to touch him in public without him first telling her to.

"Eyes down!" Ahmet ordered.

Instantly, everyone looked to the ground—all but the insolent *gengli* kneeling before him. She looked up at him, her green eyes wide. With a very naughty smile, she licked her lips for his carnal pleasure.

Ahmet was breathing hard but didn't care. He couldn't remember being as excited as he was at this moment. Meeting her gaze, he understood what she wanted to do to him.

Bianca looked up at the prince, shivering at the bold look he gave her. Slowly, he reached for his waist and pulled at the loincloth only to drop it onto the floor. His dark brows arched slightly.

Was that a challenge?

Unable to help herself, Bianca looked at his glorious cock. It was huge, a virtual weapon of impalement. Veins drew along the sides from the blunted mushroom tip. His hands were at his sides. He didn't move. Her hands were on his ass, kneading him. She couldn't stop.

Bianca glanced back up. Surely he didn't mean for her to suck his cock right here in the hall. But didn't she start it? Wasn't she the one who tried to seduce him to get out of the lashing?

Suck his giant cock or get whipped. It wasn't a hard choice. Her mouth watered.

Ahmet nodded, gesturing down his body. His eyes were hot, burning pits of fire. She saw the dark color change and shift in them, flecking with purple slivers. When she didn't move, he gestured again. It was all the permission she needed.

Why the hell not?

It wasn't like Bianca was staying in the Kingdom of…wherever she was. It wasn't like anyone would care or know that she'd given a sexy-gorgeous prince head in a hall full of people. She wanted to suck him, was excited to do so. Maybe if she pleased him, he'd take her back to his room. The idea had merit and she was more than willing to try.

Knowing everyone was there just turned Bianca on more. She liked knowing they were right there, unable to look up. According to her uploads, if they disobeyed his verbal command, they'd be killed.

The gauze of her pants adhered to her skin, stuck by the creamy juices of her needy pussy. What she wouldn't give to have someone sucking her nipples—giving the tight buds just a fraction of relief. Blazes, right now she was so horny she'd let

Prince Ahmet fuck her in front of everyone—just so long as he stuck his giant cock inside her.

Ahmet flexed his stomach ever so slightly, forcing his hips forward. Bianca knew that the subtle gesture was rare for a prince. He wasn't allowed to go to her because of some consequence her mind had yet to release to her. It excited her to know he couldn't wait, that in a small way he was defying his own laws in his need for her. Feeling very powerful with this new turn of events, she leaned forward and licked the tip. His hips jerked in reflex and she saw the smallest bead of pre-come dampening the small slit in his cock head.

Who was the submissive now?

Ahmet smelled good and tasted even better. His skin glistened with the sheen of perfumed oil. Bianca licked him again, sucking the tip of his shaft between her lips. The salty taste of his semen burst against her tongue as she licked the small hole clean. Toying with the end, she bit gently. His ass clenched beneath her hands and he shoved himself deep into her throat, nearly bruising her with his girth as he tried to dig deep. Knowing there was no way she'd fit him all in her mouth, she drew her hands forward, letting her fingernails scrape his flesh as she did so.

He kept his hands at his sides, not moving to touch her, but they did tremble and his fingers flexed as if he wanted to grab her head. Gripping the base of his cock, she began to stroke, sucking him as she worked her mouth up and down. She rolled his balls in her palms, squeezing them lightly. Only his hips worked as he thrust back and forth between her lips. Small, primal noise escaped him. When she glanced up his firm body, she saw his head was back. His mouth was open as he gasped for air. It was too much. She sucked harder, wanting to taste him, wanting him to come in her mouth so she could drink him down.

Ahmet tensed, squirting a long, hot jet of seed down her throat. He tasted sweet and she instantly swallowed him down. To her surprise, he kept thrusting and coming in a strong stream. A moan escaped her. She kept sucking, drinking furiously as she milked him dry.

When he finally finished, she dropped back onto her haunches, breathing hard. She felt strange, euphoric. Ahmet didn't move. A rainbow appeared over the marble hall. Bianca gasped, blinking as she stared at it. Her limbs felt heavy. She couldn't move.

"Livena, dress me," Prince Ahmet ordered. His voice was hoarse.

Bianca felt more than saw the woman move. Livena reached for the loincloth. Bianca growled at the woman, lurching forward to grab the material. Livena gasped. The action had been pure impulse. Unable to stop her hands, Bianca dressed the prince herself. All she knew was that she didn't want anyone else touching him.

When she'd finished, Bianca felt a hand on her arm, pulling her up. She looked at Ahmet. He didn't touch her. It was the guards who hauled her to her feet.

The prince gave her a strange look. Then, turning from her, he walked from the hall.

"The ceremony starts tonight!" the prince announced. The hall gasped in unison. His body dissolved into mist and he floated quickly away.

Bianca stiffened. As he drew away, the euphoria lessened. Out of the corner of her eye, she saw Livena. The woman was glaring at her. The guards hauled her forward, following close behind the prince. She wondered if they were going to punish her.

"Look, up there," she heard someone whisper as the prince disappeared through the doorway.

"Look."

"How...?"

"It's an omen."

Bianca didn't pay attention to the women. How could she? The guards were dragging her away. Only the look on Livena's enraged face assured her that she wasn't to be beaten. Now, if the woman had been smiling, she'd have been terrified.

"Where are we going?" Bianca asked the guards.

"Prince Ahmet wishes for you in his chambers," the one on the right answered.

"How...how do you know?" she asked.

"He ordered us," the guard on the left answered.

"But...how? He didn't say anything." Bianca, strangely eager to join the prince in his room, began to walk on her own. The guards just chuckled and didn't answer her question.

She barely noticed the plain stone walls as she was led past them. Finally, after what seemed like an eternity, she was brought to two large doors. One guard let go of her arm and opened the door. The other led her inside. She expected to see the prince. He wasn't there.

The room had a bath set up on a high pedestal. Three male servants dressed in loincloths awaited her. Their heads were shaved along the sides but long on top. The guard forced her to climb up the platform and let her go. The three slender men instantly began to undress her. Before she could so much as gasp, she was standing naked.

"Mm, beautiful," one said. The others instantly agreed.

She stepped into the warm water at their insistence, assuming they meant to leave her alone to bathe. But, as she heard splashing behind her, she tensed. She turned to see the three servants walking toward her, naked. The guard merely watched from the side.

"I can do it," Bianca said.

The servants merely smiled.

She turned to the watching guard, easily seeing his hard cock. He stared at her breasts.

"Do you mind? All of you, out. I'd like some privacy." Bianca tried to draw away from them, crossing to the opposite side of the bath. She put her hands on her hips, not at all embarrassed by her nudity. How could she be? She'd been walking around the palace in nothing but gauze anyway.

"The servants must make sure you are properly cleaned," the watching guard answered, "and I must make sure the servants remain at a proper distance. They are not to give you release."

Bianca balked, standing near the edge of the bathing pool as the servants finally reached her. The men cleaned her, rubbing their hands over her flesh, stroking her with their fingers as they soaped up her skin. She tried not to enjoy it, tried really hard, but the more they pressed, the more she was reminded of how long she'd been without sex.

Suddenly, she cursed Ahmet for leaving her like he did. She'd pleased him, sucking him dry, and he couldn't even return the favor! All she got was a bunch of servants who were forbidden from letting her find release. The one time she started to reach for her own clit, they restrained her hands.

They ran their hands over her sensitive breasts, tweaking and pinching her nipples. She moaned in pleasure. Each time they neared her clit, she tried to rub against them, but they refused to stroke her. By the time they'd finished, they all had stiff erections. Her mind said they would do—*any* cock would do so long as it filled her and rode her good. But, just thinking of it, her pussy didn't seem to ache so much.

No, her body wanted Ahmet. It was his giant cock she wanted to pry her open, his body she wanted pounding into her. It was his seed she wanted spilled, his hands on her breasts, his mouth kissing her. Sexual energy charged the air. She was a bundle of nerves.

"He will be pleased," the guard said.

"Yes, very pleased," a servant agreed. They backed away from her, all of them staring at her naked, flushed skin.

Bianca looked at them, confused.

"Her energy is great," the guard continued.

Bianca snorted. She didn't know about energy, but if she didn't find release soon, she'd go mad. And the first ass she was going to kick in her newfound insanity was Prince Ahmet's.

* * * * *

Bianca was pissed when the three servants left her unfulfilled. They stoked the damned fire, the least they could do was put out the flames. Instead, they handed her a towel, brushed her hair, rubbed her with oil and dressed her, sending her on her merry way. She ached with sexual frustration and it took all her energy to keep upright as she walked between the guards. They led her to a bedchamber, pushing her inside before shutting the door.

"Did you enjoy yourself?"

Bianca turned to the large bed in the middle of the room. She didn't answer. Prince Ahmet lay on the mattress, watching her through seductively narrowed eyes. He was naked and apparently completely comfortable with the fact. Though, with his tightly muscled body and thick cock, there was definitely no reason for him to be ashamed. His legs were crossed leisurely at the ankles, his erection thick and ready for her, standing tall between his thighs.

The prince sat up, looking concerned. "You did not enjoy my gift, *gengli*?"

"Gift?" Bianca frowned. Was this guy crazy? "What gift?"

"The bathers," the prince said, frowning. "Did they not bathe you? Touch you?"

"Oh, I see." Bianca stepped toward the bed. She placed her hands on her hips. The thick material of the towel was soft against her skin and it didn't help her sexual frustration that she was naked beneath it. Scowling, she glared at the prince. "So you think getting felt up by three guys and then being denied any sort of release is a gift?"

No wonder the women run away from you.

"I don't understand. You have no wish to be touched?" Prince Ahmet really did look confused. He crawled forward on the bed.

Bianca shivered. He truly was a handsome man. She did wish to be touched, but not by the men in the bath. She wanted to be touched by him.

The prince smiled. "Ah, I understand. Come, you may release me now. Then you will feel better."

Bianca stared at him. She really, really wanted to take him up on his offer, but something inside her held back. She looked at his cock, remembering the feel of it in her mouth, the taste of it when he came. It took all her resolve, but she managed, "Ah, no thanks. I'm good."

The prince frowned. "I said you could release me."

"And I said no." Bianca moved, her legs aching, her pussy throbbing with need. She walked around the chamber, looking around at the draped silks and intricate carvings. Then, seeing a window, she looked at the bright, mountainous landscape. The room was high on a mountain, overlooking a lush valley filled with trees. Two yellow suns shone down from the purple-tinted sky, one on each side of a larger moon. The trees were almost red, surrounded by large green flowers with burgundy stems. She wasn't one for flowers, but they were beautiful. The breeze cooled her wet hair, making her shiver. "Lovely view you have here."

As she turned, a white mist appeared before her and the prince materialized in front of her, blocking her view of the landscape. He stood, not touching her as he said, "You can release me now. You have my permission."

"Ah, tempting offer, but no." Bianca moved away from him. He lifted his hand as if he would restrain her, but he held back, balling his fingers into a tight fist. Outside, the sound of lightning crashed and it began to rain, hard. The sound of it hit over the room. The room grew dark and the light all but disappeared from outside the window. Instead of being frightened by the sudden weather change, Bianca thought it pretty.

"But, before…" He looked confused. "You do not wish to drink of me again?"

Oh, easy there, Mr. Arrogance.

Bianca thought of her mission. Well, she'd never really been one to do what she was told to. She made a move for the door, turning her back on him. If this man had any more ego, she'd be knocked off the planet. "I think I'll just go release myself."

As she reached out to open it, the mist formed in front of her. Her hand met the prince's tight stomach and she jerked it back. She didn't want to be reminded how hot his flesh was or how good his cock felt in her mouth.

"I do not understand. Do you wish for me to send for others to watch you please me?" Ahmet asked, lifting his hand, only to draw it away.

Bianca thought about that. She didn't know what had come over her in the hall. But now, the idea of someone coming to join them just made her angry. She didn't want to share the prince. She placed her hands on her hips, very aware of how naked he was. "Um, tempting, but no thanks. Why don't you go get another one of your little *genglis*?"

The poor man did look genuinely lost at her dismissal. His expression was open to her as he studied her. "I don't understand. Why do you not wish to stay with me? I am a prince, descendent of the gods. Your being here is a great honor. Have you no wish to please me?"

"What don't you understand?" Bianca asked. "Is it so hard to conceive that a woman would want someone other than you in her bed?"

"Ah, but you do desire me," he countered. Again his hand lifted. This time the fingers, almost hesitantly, glanced over her cheek. He withdrew his touch just as quickly. She didn't move. "Why do you do this?"

"Mm, yeah, you're handsome and all, prince," Bianca said. "But to tell you the truth, I have no desire to bed a man who just lies there. It's kind of boring if you know what I mean."

He frowned. Obviously, he didn't.

"What would you think if I merely lay down on the bed, my legs spread—"

"I would enjoy it," he answered quickly.

"—staring at the ceiling as you did all the work, not touching you, not kissing you, not—"

"I would not enjoy it," he admitted, more reluctantly than before.

"There's your answer." Bianca made a move as if she would push past him. "Now, if you don't mind, I—"

"But I had the bathers, they—"

"Ah, then I should desire the bathers," Bianca said. "They aroused me. They shall finish me. Thank you for the wonderful suggestion. Excuse me."

The prince frowned. "I aroused you. I ordered them to—"

Her look cut him off. "No, they touched me, they aroused me. That's how it works. In fact, you had nothing to do with it."

Okay, that was a lie. She'd been thinking about him the entire time she was in the bath. But this arrogant prince really didn't need to know that.

"You're a strange woman."

"Is that supposed to be a compliment? It's a wonder any women come to your bed at all." Lowering her voice, she mocked him, "Come and pleasure me. Release me. It's all about me. Me. Me. Me. M—"

The prince stopped her by lifting his hand to her face. He touched her lightly. She waited as he traced over her jaw, moving his hand down to the towel wrapped around her body. Slowly, he hooked his finger between her breasts and tugged. It fell to the floor.

He devoured her with his eyes before moving to touch her with his hands. Cupping her breasts, he massaged them gently. A soft moan escaped him as he touched her.

"You're so soft." Ahmet took an aggressive step forward, walking her back toward his bed. He moved his fingers over her hips only to come back up her stomach to her breasts. "Is this what you're asking for?"

Bianca shivered. Oh, yeah. That's definitely what she'd been asking for. His hands seemed to hesitate. She knew the man was on foreign territory. In the past, he'd not moved to touch a woman, give her pleasure.

"Mm, yes," she whispered, encouraging him. He smiled. His exploration grew bolder, his touch more sure.

With a light toss, he lifted her beneath the arms and threw her back on the bed. Bianca gasped, wiggling against the mattress in arousal. Starting at her feet, he massaged her, roaming over her as a white mist. The mist was everywhere at once—along her legs, near her pussy, covering her breasts. It felt as if a million fingers softly probed her flesh, she arched and moaned. Everywhere the mist touched, she tingled.

When he again formed into a solid man, he loomed over her. His thighs spread, trapping her down. He grinned. Bianca moved restlessly against the mattress, trying to touch him.

"Don't move, I am enjoying this." When he looked at her, his eyes were nearly completely purple as they glowed with a strange light.

Ahmet continued to touch her, seeming to find pleasure in watching her respond to him. He found her neck with his lips, biting and kissing a trail down her throat to her breasts. Licking her nipples, he lapped them with his tongue only to bite them gently. The caress shot straight from her breasts to her soaked cunt, causing her to nearly come from just the sensation of need.

"Ah, okay, that's enough." Unable to hold back, Bianca tried to urge him to move so he could come inside her, trying to work her legs so they were on the outside of his thighs. His muscles gripped, keeping her from her goal. She knew he was strong, but the sheer power of him was amazing.

Bianca moaned in frustration. If she didn't find release soon, her whole body was going to explode. The way she felt, so wet, so tense, so fucking hot, the explosion would probably knock out the whole kingdom. He resisted her grasping hands and wiggling body.

"Mm, please, Ahmet."

"I like when you beg me. Beg me more." He kissed a trail down her stomach. His legs dissolved, only to reappear between her thighs, pushing her wide open.

"That is so not fair," she said. He chuckled, a deliciously wicked sound.

"I always wanted to taste a climax. When I checked to see if you were taken by my brothers, I got a taste of your cream." Ahmet flicked his tongue over her swollen clit, as if testing her. She tensed beneath him, gasping loudly. "Mm, it is good."

Bianca's eyes rolled in her head. The man might never have done this before, but he was saying and doing all the right things.

"You're not begging," he said, quirking a brow. "Do you not want it?"

Oh, he didn't play fair. He knew damned well she wanted it. Although he was the future king and trying this whole giving a woman pleasure thing for the first time. What the blazes? She could beg.

"Ahmet," she moaned, wiggling as she pushed her thighs wide. His hot gaze devoured her body. "Please, I beg of you, touch me with your mouth. Lick my pussy for me. Bury your face in it until I come all over you."

He flicked her again. It was a lightly teasing caress. Sticking her finger along her folds, she got it wet with her cream and drew it to her lips. Bianca affected a pout. "Mm, don't you want to taste me?"

Ahmet's purple eyes darkened a shade. He growled, instantly submerging his face in her wet cunt, aggressively drinking her cream.

Bianca nearly screamed at the force and enthusiasm in which he worked his mouth. He gripped her sides and pulled her down on the bed, angling her hips up toward his face. Her legs flailed in the air as she gripped at the bedspread. He willingly moved his mouth, excitedly probing at her clit before delving his hot tongue inside her. If she wasn't mistaken, his tongue dissolved into mist, reaching high up inside her. The tingling it left behind was unmistakable.

"Ah, yes," she cried, moving her slit against his mouth, her body racked with need. From the moment she first saw him, she wanted him. Everything about him turned her on—his hard body, his stubborn arrogance, the sound of his low voice. "Ah, just like that."

Bianca gasped, unable to so much as scream as she came hard against his mouth. He kept working, drinking up her orgasm. Her hold on the bed weakened. He pulled so hard on her thighs that he fell back as she let go.

Bianca was a mass of nerves, unable to move from her spot on the gigantic bed. She breathed hard, feeling Ahmet dissolve into mist to untangle their limbs. When he reappeared, he was by her side. He pressed his lips to her throat.

"Is that what you wanted?"

Bianca couldn't believe that a man as arrogant, as confident as he would be shy, but he did sound as if he sought her approval. Slowly, she nodded her head. "Oh, yeah, prince. That will do just fine."

Chapter Three

Ahmet studied the woman before him in wonder. She had the most beautiful blonde hair and green eyes, which sparkled with an almost magical depth. His cock was still hard, and yet he felt somehow satisfied with himself, knowing what he'd done had pleased her. Smiling, he knew he wanted to please her again.

Ahmet had been with many women, but none had dared to defy him. Strangely, he liked being defied and challenged. He liked knowing a woman wanted more from him than just to sleep with a descendent of the gods. In fact, this woman seemed unconcerned with who he was. She'd tried to strike him twice, rebelled against his commands, denied him and gave him more pleasure than he'd ever remembered receiving. He liked how she passionately said his name in her low, sweet voice, not bothering with his title.

Ever since he first saw her, he wanted her, could think of no others in his bed. He had others in his bed—many others. Deciding that a minute was enough of a break, Ahmet pushed up from the mattress. He'd seen what some of the women did to each other to entertain him. Now it would be his turn to try. "What is your name, *gengli*?"

"Mm, Bianca," she answered quietly. Her eyes were closed. He wanted them to open again.

Dissolving himself, he moved beside her. Then, grabbing her body, he flipped her onto her stomach.

"Ah, what…?" she began weakly.

"I want to please you more." Ahmet jerked her hips up, pulling her ass into the air. The sweet smell of her pussy beckoned him. This time, when he stroked her, he used his finger, thrusting it along the rim of her slit. Her body came to life once more and she moaned, rocking back onto his hand. Almost instantly, she covered him with cream. He grinned, letting his fingers glide in and out. She moaned, weakly pushing back. "Does this please you?"

"Mm, yes," Bianca groaned. "Ah, please, I want your cock. I need you to fuck me. Please, fuck me."

Ahmet smiled, for it was what he wanted also.

* * * * *

Bianca was near the breaking point. Ahmet moved behind her, holding her hips. He kept her ass angled to him. She tensed, knowing he'd soon be thrusting his huge cock inside her. Nerves bound her stomach, knowing how big he was, how very thick, but she was too aroused to back out now.

He teased her with his tip, letting the blunted head glide up and down over her wet slit, probing just along her entrance without thrusting in. It had been so long since she'd been fucked. She needed it, needed him to give it to her. Bianca wanted him to fuck every hole in her body. She wanted to bathe in his come. She wanted to suck him dry.

"Ask me again to fuck you," he said.

"Ah, yes, please fuck me. Give me your big cock." Bianca couldn't think, didn't care that she begged him. She thrust her hips back, trying to slip him inside. A weak sound left her throat as she missed. He continued to stroke his cock head up and down her pussy. "Fuck me, Ahmet."

"It pleases me to have you say my name like that."

"Ahmet," she moaned, breathy. She felt him jerk. Every nerve in her body was centered on his touch. "Ahmet."

This time when he probed her, he didn't stop. He eased himself in, taking it slow as he pried her body apart. Pleasure-pain built inside her at his size, but she wanted it all, wanted his cock filling her to the hilt. Bianca groaned, her entire body exploding with pleasure. Her legs spread wider, trying to make room.

"You are small," he said, the words a groan. He stopped pushing and she could tell he hadn't fitted himself inside her completely. "I have no wish to hurt you."

"Don't stop, oh, please don't stop." Using all her strength, she pushed back, embedding his cock deep within her. She groaned in approval, matching his throaty growl. "Ahmet, yeah, baby, just like that. Ride me."

Bianca writhed in pleasure as he obeyed, using her hips to control the thrusts. He worked back and forth, gliding in her cream. The tension built and she tried not to climax too fast because she didn't want the sensations to stop. Reaching between her legs, she rubbed her clit. It was too much.

Her pussy clamped down on him hard, squeezing his cock as she came. Ahmet grunted and jerked. He sprayed hot come inside her, filling her with his essence. Her thighs were sticky and wet as he pulled himself from her. The room smelled of sex.

"Again," he said. "I will bring you pleasure again."

Bianca, on the verge of falling sated to the bed, turned to glance over her shoulder. His hands on her hips kept her from moving.

"No, like this." His words were low, wicked with promise. She felt his cock, still wet with their climax, drawing along her ass. He spread her cheeks wide, moving along her tight rosette. "I will give you pleasure here now."

Her heart beat a furious rhythm. Her body was still stirred from her last orgasm and she was ready for even more. She felt him pushing, rimming her ass with his thumb to prepare her body for him. She tensed. The nerves inside her rectum pulsed to life.

Bianca couldn't see it, but she could feel that his cock was aroused, thick against her body. She'd never heard of a man that could recover so fast. It shouldn't have been possible.

Ahmet thrust forward, working in shallow thrusts as he broke her open to him. Mist surrounded her, as his hands dissolved to slide over her flesh, caressing her breasts and stomach at once. Before she could think, she was pushing her body onto him, letting him ride her as he slid within her body.

Ahmet made grunting noises as he took her. The mist of him glided down to her slit, probing up inside her pussy as he sent wave after wave of tingling sensation through her. It was too much. She came again, arching her back as she climaxed. His howl of pleasure soon joined hers as he climaxed inside her ass.

When the trembling subsided, he let her go. Bianca fell on the bed, instantly exhausted. She couldn't move, couldn't speak. Her heart pounded violently, filling her ears until she couldn't hear. Sleep came for her and she couldn't even think to fight it.

Ahmet lay next to Bianca as she fell asleep. He felt her drifting into the land of dreams and smiled. He was sated, renewed. Unlike her, he wasn't at all tired. Sex replenished his powers, made him strong. And if the feeling in his limbs was any indication, Bianca had renewed him well beyond the pleasure of a thousand harem women.

He called the guards to him, able to give them commands with his mind, though they could not answer back. He would have her watched so that no harm came to her while she slept. Some of the harem women were missing. In truth, it was possible they merely left the palace, as they were not forced to stay there. But usually, they would tell someone. Lately, they'd just been leaving without word. When guards were sent to their villages, it was said the women had not gone back. It worried him enough to contact the outside world for help in the matter, though he had yet to receive word back as to whether or not they'd take his case.

Slipping up from the bed to let Bianca rest, he grinned. If he were to stay next to her, his power would grow and disturb her sleep. He glanced over her naked back—her hair spilled in a wild, tangled mess over her shoulders. She was beautiful.

First, he would bathe, and then he would see to his kingdom. Ahmet glanced out the window. The rain had stopped and a rainbow stretched across the sky. The sun shone brightly, giving life to his planet. If he didn't already feel the evidence of her power inside him, the weather was proof. He'd found his queen.

* * * * *

Bianca moaned, feeling the bed shift. She tried to lift her head but she was too tired. Ahmet's touch had left her drained. Suddenly, a cold metal clamp seized her wrists, followed by a clamp on her ankles. She jerked awake, blinking as she was flipped over onto her naked back.

Livena stood above her with her two guards. Hands on hips, the woman glared at her. "I will be his queen, not you. I have been here the longest. I am the one."

Bianca stiffened, ready to scream in protest, but a gag was thrust between her lips. How could she have forgotten the threat to the harem girls? How could she have forgotten her mission? The answer washed over her in a rush. Ahmet. She felt him inside her still. She didn't know how, but she was connected to him.

Livena motioned the guards to go to the door. Bianca was lifted over a brawny shoulder. The man clamped his hand down on her naked ass, squeezing tight. She fought him, landing a kick to his gut. The man grunted in displeasure but didn't let go as he sprinted down the hall. Bianca saw the other guard behind them, running as well. Livena held back, turning to go down the hall toward the harem.

* * * * *

Ahmet stiffened, coming up in the bathing pool. Bianca was in trouble. Somehow, he felt that she was. He didn't have time to contemplate the obvious connection he had to her. With one great leap, he jumped from the water onto the marble floor. Running, wet and naked, he raced through the stone halls. He first checked his bedchamber. She wasn't there. Using his mind, he ordered all the guards to be on alert. Outside it started to rain, thundering as a torrent of water was released from the sky.

* * * * *

Bianca let her body become dead weight as she conserved her energy. Everything she'd learned about survival when training as an RLS-69 kicked in full force. She watched, memorizing the turns they took as they wound through an endless maze of hallways. Suddenly, the guard stopped and waited as his friend pushed a stone on the wall. Her jaw stiffened as she watched the wall open up. A part of her wanted to fight, to run, as they stepped inside the wall, but she knew she had to see where they were taking her. This was her mission and she didn't have much of a choice but to do it.

Bianca heard the wall shut behind as they walked down a long spiral staircase. Soon, murmuring voices sounded, growing louder as they descended. The guard stopped, depositing her on the stone floor.

Bianca's arms were heavy with the weight of her manacles. She looked around. Brilliant colored silk draped over the stone walls. The room was filled with women, all who turned to look at her arrival.

Bianca frowned. There were at least a hundred women in the room, possibly more, most of them dressed in gauze outfits. Without having to ask, she knew they were the missing harem women. They weren't dead, merely held prisoner by a crazy woman who would be queen. A pang of jealousy hit her as she realized Prince Ahmet had slept with all of them.

"What's going on?" Bianca demanded. She was still completely naked.

The guard smiled, reaching to undo her manacles. "You will be safe here until Prince Ahmet chooses his queen. Don't worry."

Bianca rubbed her wrists. "Who? Livena? Don't you think he'd already have chosen her if he was going to?"

The guard frowned. The second guard came forward and handed her a bundle of silk. Bianca wrapped it around her body before stepping closer to him.

"What do you think will happen to you when the prince finds out what you've done here? Do you think he'll reward you for stealing his women before he was done with them?" Bianca shook her head, affecting a sad look of pity. "Is Livena really so good in bed that you'd be willing to risk the future king's wrath?"

"Death?" the guard asked. "We will not be killed. When Livena is queen, we will be rewarded and you all will be let go."

"Are you really so foolish?" Bianca laughed.

"It's no use." Bianca turned to look at the woman who spoke. She had brassy red hair and wide green eyes. "They're drugged."

The guard turned to go. Bianca moved to sit by the redhead.

"I'm Greta," the redhead said.

"I'm Bianca." She heard the guard leave. "What do you mean drugged?"

"You're not from here, are you?" Greta asked.

"You're the first to notice."

"Well, you know." Greta shrugged. "I was shipwrecked. We aliens tend to recognize our own."

"What do you mean drugged?"

"From what I can tell, these men feed off of sexual energy. Livena has somehow harnessed that energy and has those two under her complete control. There's no use in talking to them. They're pussy-whipped."

Bianca chuckled. "What about escape?"

Greta frowned. "There's like a hundred of us down here. Don't you think we'd have escaped if there was a way?"

"Good point." Bianca stood. She made a move to the stairs.

"Wait, didn't you listen to a thing I said? There's no way out."

"Maybe not for you," Bianca said. Then, lower, under her breath, she added, "But then you're not a trained Red Light Specialist."

* * * * *

Ahmet strode through the hallways, reaching out with his powers for Bianca. He knew instinctively she wouldn't have left him. She couldn't have. She was his queen. He was connected to her.

Feeling his way along the hall, he stopped. Bianca was close. He touched the wall, creeping along the old stone. There were many old passageways hidden behind the castle walls, many of them forgotten with time.

"Bianca?" he asked, stopping. He ran his hands over the rock.

"Ahmet?" The yell was faint, but he could tell it was her. "Press…rock… stone…women."

He frowned, running his hands over the wall. Seeing a crack, he dissolved, slinking through it. Bianca was on the other side. She jumped to see him.

"I found you," he said.

"Hm," Bianca answered. "How about you find your way back out and open up this door? Third stone from the small one, two down."

Ahmet moved to touch her, wanting to touch her again. His flesh was all too eager to remember the pleasures touching her brought him. Why had he never moved to touch women before? He'd always been told that he couldn't bend to someone lower than him in station. Since he was future king, all were lower to him—all but his queen. "I knew I'd find you."

She flinched, jerking away from him. Scowling, she said, "Yeah, and I found your girlfriends. They're waiting for you, stud."

Ahmet blinked. Was she jealous? "Girlfriends?"

"Let me introduce myself, stud," Bianca said. "Agent Bianca, Red Light Specialist, sent here to find your missing harem women."

She was the agent being sent to help him? He frowned. It couldn't be. Though it would explain her strange ways.

Bianca pointed down the stairwell. "Missing harem women are there. Livena is your culprit. She's used sex to entrance the two harem guards into helping her. I just earned my freedom. Case closed. Solving this case in a day has to be a company record. Maybe I'll get a nice little plaque with my name on it. Doesn't every girl want the skies to part and bugs to drop in their honor? Now, if you wouldn't mind, float on through there and open up the door."

Ahmet stiffened. She had not come to the palace to be with him. She never had sought to give him pleasure. He moved to touch her and drew back. Slowly, he nodded, misting through the door. Following her instructions, he pushed the stone. The door opened and she stepped through.

"I'd say my work here is done. I'm going to go contact my director and get out of here. Nice knowing you, prince." Bianca walked away, her steps angry and hard as she moved.

Ahmet called the guards with his mind, directing them to free the girls and to take Livena into custody.

He moved to follow Bianca, catching up to her easily in mist form. Stopping before her, he solidified and blocked her way.

Bianca frowned, still insanely jealous over the hundred women this man had called lovers. She pushed at his arm. He grabbed her wrist. She tried to pull away, he tugged her closer.

"What exactly is it you want?" she demanded.

"To pleasure you." He turned on his heels. Bianca tried to protest, but he didn't listen as he dragged her behind him to the bathing pools. He dropped the loincloth from his waist as he walked. Then, stopping, he turned to her and began working on her silk covering.

Bianca swatted at his hands. "Hey, what do you think you are doing? You have a basement full of women just waiting to please you."

"You are jealous."

Damn right she was jealous! Bianca frowned. "No. Why would I be?"

"It pleases me that you are jealous."

"It would please me to drown you," Bianca returned, pointing at the bath.

"All right." Ahmet grabbed her arm and jumped, pulling her under with him. She screamed before dipping under the surface. Before she could get to air, his lips were on hers, kissing her. They broke surface, his hands on her breast, pinching her nipple.

Bianca cried out. It felt so good. She wanted to protest, wanted to stay angry, but couldn't. He glided his hands over her flesh, stroking every inch of her body until she was as aroused as he was. His hard cock pressed into her stomach as he trapped her along the bathing pool's wall.

"This isn't fighting fair," she whispered in between panting breaths. Her only answer was his low chuckle.

Taking her by her hips, Ahmet lifted her, angling his body to enter her. With a hard, claiming stroke, he delved inside her depths, stretching her pussy wide to accept him. Bianca cried out in pleasure as he filled her completely.

"Does this please you?" he asked.

"Ah, yes, Ahmet, yes." Bianca rocked her hips, meeting him stroke for stroke as he pumped into her hard. "Ah, yes, fuck me!"

Her back pressed along the hard, wet stone but she didn't care. He felt too good inside her. He touched her breasts and kissed her mouth until she was mindless in her need for him. The tension built in her body.

"Ah, yeah!" she cried.

"Tell me I pleasure you," he said.

"Ah, yes, Ahmet, you pleasure me!" Bianca wrapped her legs around his strong waist, urging him deeper.

"Tell me you are jealous."

"Yes, yes, I'm jealous. Ah, yeah, deeper. Fuck me harder!"

"Tell me you are my queen."

Bianca didn't think. "Yes, I'm your queen. I'm your queen, Ahmet. Don't stop. Don't ever stop!"

"No!"

The high-pitched cry sounded just as Bianca's body racked with her climax. It took a moment for the sound to register. The pleasure of her orgasm was too great. Ahmet thrust several more times before he too exploded with release. His hot come filled her womb, heating her even more.

"No!" Livena repeated from the doorway. "You can't be! I am to be queen! Me!"

Ahmet pulled Bianca closer to him. He was breathing hard when he looked at the harem mistress. She wrapped her arms around his back, also turning to look.

"This is my queen. She is mine," Ahmet said. "It is done."

Bianca gasped. Two guards came to take the kicking and screaming Livena away. As they left, they said, "Congratulations, Prince Ahmet."

Bianca ignored the men. "What did you just say?"

"That you are my wife and a future queen?" he asked, frowning. "You said you were. It is done. You accepted me and—"

"Ah, wait a minute… I…" She tired to squirm away from him. He frowned, pressing closer. She felt a curious warmth inside her. She wanted his words to be true. This was too strange. He was her charge.

"You are mine," he stated. "You give me too much pleasure, *gengli*."

He really needed to stop calling her a whore. "You know, calling your wife that isn't very flattering."

"What? *Gengli*? But you are the most beautiful woman I've ever laid eyes on."

"Oh, is that what that means?" she asked, smiling. He nodded. It was insane, but being with Ahmet just felt so right. She could feel him inside her and just knew. He was the one. Surely Director Simon would let her stay. Her mission was completed. She was a free woman. "Okay, you can call me that. But we will be discussing this little harem of yours. There are going to be some major changes around her, Prince Ahmet, starting with your—"

Ahmet kissed her, cutting off her words. When he pulled back, he asked, "Fine. Done. The harem is no more. I do not need it for my energy. Can I pleasure you now, my Princess?"

Bianca rolled her eyes at her godlike husband. She saw a rainbow forming overhead. Giggling, she said, "Sure, if you must."

Ahmet proceeded to make love to her through the long night. As they came together, she felt their hearts joining along with their bodies. Somehow, Bianca just knew this was her destiny and everything was going to work out just fine.

Part Three
Sonja

Chapter One

Agent Sonja had been walking for what felt like years. She knew the A-mac wasn't supposed to spit her out where she could be seen, but putting her a week away from her target was a little overly cautious in her opinion. Not to mention she was in the middle of a thick jungle filled with wild animals, surrounded by alien plant life.

And, oh, was it hot and humid! She'd been sleeping on the hard ground and her back was sore from it. The pain only made her all the more irritable. Her clothing stuck to her skin and all she wanted was a real bath with lots and lots of bubbles. Aside from an occasional rain, she hadn't been able to properly bathe.

The last thing she thought she'd be doing when she signed on for Simon's little rehabilitation project was trekking through nature. Sonja wasn't a nature kind of girl. She wasn't really a trekking kind of girl. Hell, before RLS-69, she wasn't a "go out on a mission" kind of girl. She liked nice things like water baths and meals eaten at an actual table — or anywhere that wasn't out in the wilderness. She liked wearing clean clothes and smelling like perfume. So what if she was a little on the prissy side? There wasn't anything wrong with enjoying basic comforts.

"Things change," Sonja mumbled, pushing back the sweaty strands of her hair. She knew she had to be getting close.

At least the A-mac had given her hiking boots and a pair of really sturdy pants. No doubt because Abbi had helped in her travel arrangements. Sonja really liked that piece of A.I. hardware. Simon would have selected something a bit more provocative and she didn't see trying to hike in a two-piece teddy and a thong up her ass. The black tank top and jacket suited her well enough, as did the fully stocked backpack.

Still, she knew some of the women got sent to cushy palaces. Why couldn't she go to a palace? Or a hotel with room service? Yeah, room service. She'd order fried sea slugs smothered in white sauce, *ginlo* bread, *laber* roast and a pile of Lithorian chocolate.

Hey, it was a dream, why not dream big?

Sonja's stomach growled. Instead of chocolate, she'd be having dried meat chunks and rainwater she'd collected from the big leaves—again. Anyway she looked at it, this mission sucked. Big time.

Something buzzed past her ear several times and she swatted at it. The insects on this planet were ridiculous in size. If one offered to carry her backpack, she was leaving. The buzzing sounded again, only this time she felt whatever it was land on her shoulder. With her fast reflexes, Sonja smacked it and instantly felt sticky goo beneath her hand.

Pulling her hand back down, Sonja found the remains of a greenish purple bug. When she recognized its stinger, she sighed. "Ahh, just great! Simon sends me to the middle of nowhere and they *still* have *gelipson* bugs here. If I get stung and swell up like a balloon, I'm so demanding sick pay. Wait, that's right, I don't get paid."

Seeing a dense overhang, she grabbed a knife from behind her back and swung her arm back and forth to get through it. According to the information downloaded into her head, if she made noise as she walked, none of the local animals would bother her. So far it had worked. The only animal she'd seen was some sort of large bird that followed her as she walked. But, just in case, her backpack had been equipped with a special repellant. Sonja dumped it on her head hourly.

Feeling her gooey fingers, she mumbled, "It obviously doesn't repel bugs."

Aside from the walking, her mission was simple. She had to find some man named Pacal and convince him, by any means necessary, that he was supposed to do whatever was on the paper she carried. Not for the first time, she cursed the fact that she couldn't read the paper she carried. Apparently, she could speak this man's language, she just couldn't read it.

"Simon, come on!" she growled, swinging her knife harder. Talking to herself was better than the strange noises of the jungle. "Bugs, nature, sweat, walking? Just so I can be some kind of exotic postman? The universe does have courier services that will do this really cheap."

In some of her darker moments, while huddled near a campfire in a world that turned the pitchest of blacks, she thought maybe the paper held her own death warrant. Several times she thought of throwing it into the fire. She could just imagine getting there only to find that Pacal had been ordered to kill her.

Okay, she wasn't exactly on a hit list. In fact, she'd been doing time on Restigatio for public lewdness. Her ex-boyfriend slipped some pills into her soda and the next thing she remembered was waking up in prison. According to her file, she'd danced naked on a table and told some political dignitary to suck her cock.

Sonja frowned. Why in the world would she say to suck her cock? It's not like she had a cock to suck. It's not like she'd ever had a cock growing from her body that could've once upon a time been sucked. Nope, she was all female. But, according to thirty witnesses, that's exactly what she'd said.

Apparently, the dignitary was a religious fanatic and she'd hurt his delicate sensibilities. The fact that Charles, the good for nothing ex, had slipped her a hallucinogen didn't seem to matter. She was convicted before waking up the next morning. Lucky for her, the little table dance was all that happened. It could've been much, much worse.

She swung, chopping and hacking at the brush. Suddenly, her knife hit stone with a heavy clink. Sonja stopped. Frowning, she cut at the thick mass of vines, uncovering a large statue.

"Not a very attractive race, are you?" she mused, eyeing the figure. It was that of a warrior, his arms drawn in as he held a shield. The shield was carved into the shape of a bird. The warrior's stone feet were as wide as his hips and head, making him very square shaped. The wide shoulders directed her gaze, forcing it up and then back down the statue.

Maybe she'd been too hasty in her assessment as to the race's looks, because she sure the hell had a hard time looking away. Of course, wondering what the statue's cock size was didn't help. She really, really needed to get laid.

Leaning closer to examine it, she swore. Sonja could see a nick in the stone leg where she'd hit it with the knife. Lucky for her, no one was around to arrest her for vandalism. She did not want to go back to Restigatio.

The information embedded inside her head told her she was close to Tenoc Temple. Nerves bunched in her stomach as she marched past the statue. She swung her arm, cutting at the vines as she slowly progressed. Suddenly, her knife sliced nothing but air and she was free of the thick overhanging.

Sonja emerged from the jungle, stepping onto the stone walkway before a great temple. The structure was high, with easily a hundred steps leading up from the rectangular base. Instead of forming a pyramid, the structure had a flat top with what looked like doors leading inside. There was only one path up and that was the stairs before her. The other sides appeared to be steep and smooth. Stone snake heads protruded along the bottom ridge, their mouths open wide. More humanoid statues lined the walk up.

Such a warm welcome.

She expected to find guards, someone, anyone. The temple looked abandoned. Hearing a squawk, she looked over. Her friend the bird perched nearby. Its blue feathers ruffled. Automatically, she reached into her pack and pulled out a piece of meat. She tossed it at the animal. He caught it in his beak and flew off.

After her journey, Sonja didn't relish climbing the temple stairs. But according to her information, Pacal would be at the top of this monstrous structure. The sooner she saw him, the sooner she'd be off this bug-infested jungle and set free—hopefully.

* * * * *

Sonja sighed, wiping her forehead as she finally neared the last step. She was so high, she could see over the top of the jungle. It went on forever, reaching over the distance like a sea of green. Shrugging off her pack, she looked around. No one was there to greet her.

Great. Just her luck, it would be abandoned. Maybe this wasn't Tenoc. Maybe she'd taken a wrong turn. It wasn't like the damn planet had road signs posted on various trees.

"No, this has to be it," she said to herself, sitting down on the top step. As soon as she caught her breath, she'd go inside. But for the moment, she wanted nothing more than to rest.

Hearing a squawk close to her back, she slowly turned. Her bird friend landed on the platform. Sonja eyed him, reaching for her pack. She might as well feed the meat to the animal because she was sick of eating it. The bird was close, closer than he'd ever come. She reached out her hand, the meat in her palm. The bird took it but didn't fly off. It craned its neck forward. Slowly, she petted its soft, blue feathers.

"Amazing."

Sonja tensed at the low, gravelly word. Just the sound of it made an odd tingle in her nipples. The bird squawked and flew off. She quickly got to her feet. There was no one there. "Hello?"

"Here," came a voice. Sonja looked to the entrance of the temple. The square door was decorated with small pieces of turquoise. As she watched, a man emerged from the shadows. He wore a turquoise mask with bright white teeth made from shells. Dark eyes moved beneath the eye holes. Atop his head was a headdress of bright blue feathers, spanning up in an arch from one ear to the other.

Sonja could see his long dark hair beneath the headdress. It was braided, hanging nearly to the man's ass. His chest looked broad, strong, even bigger than the stone statue at the base of the stairs. He wore a sleeveless poncho that reached to his feet. The off-white material looked soft and clean. It was decorated with fine, braided patterns of bright colors along the bottom edge. The braid work matched the belt around his waist.

His arms were bare, except for the thick bands of black tattoos around his biceps. Muscles bulged his flesh, flexing as he moved. He didn't wear pants under the long poncho. Leather sandals with braided wool straps were on his feet.

Sonja was at a loss for words. There was definitely something powerful and erotic to the man—his hidden face, the ceremonial robes. All the carefully planned introductions left her as she said one word, "Pacal."

"You know me?" he answered. His voice made her spine tingle and her knees weak.

"You are Pacal?"

"You are at my temple, are you not?" He turned from her and walked inside.

Sonja frowned, coming to her senses as he left her alone. She made a move to follow him, grabbing her pack. Inside, the temple was all stone. Large columns, carved with knot work, held the ceiling from the smooth floor. Fires burned in ceremonial urns on platforms.

"Pacal?" Sonja called, not seeing him. She walked slowly, looking around. "Excuse me?"

"Here."

"Oh," Sonja blinked, seeing movement at the end of the long hall. She moved forward, glancing around to make sure they were alone. They were. The downloads kicked in and she stopped before him. He sat atop a throne. Skulls were carved up the sides. She squinted to see them in the firelight, realizing that maybe they weren't carved of stone, but real human skulls. She swallowed, nervous. Bowing down on one leg, she said meekly, "Forgive me, Pacal, I did not know you."

"Who but I would be here?"

"I was told you would have guards," she said, not looking up. Her eyes bored into the floor, seeing fine cracks in the cement. Being so high up allowed a breeze to sweep over the temple hall from outside.

"So I do."

Sonja frowned. She glanced to the sides, trying not to be obvious. She saw no one.

"Now that you have found me, what do you want with me?" He sounded bored.

"I've come to give you a message." In her precarious position, her backpack became heavy. Until he gave her permission, she couldn't stand. Outside the temple hall, her rudeness may be forgiven, but inside was another matter. She knew if she stood too soon, she'd be killed. He could leave her kneeling for a decade if he so wished.

After what seemed like an eternity, he said, "You may rise and give me your name."

Sonja relaxed, taking a deep breath. "Sonja."

"Sonja," he said, nodding. She couldn't see his expression beneath the mask, and quite frankly he looked frightening studying her from his throne. "First you must bathe and dress as befitting this temple. I will forgive your insult of coming in here thus, but only because of the Grafowk."

Grafowk? Grafowk? She searched her mind. *What is that again?*

"They do not just let anyone pet them."

The bird! Her life had been spared by a bird. She was suddenly very thankful the thing had followed her.

Pacal stood, motioning her to do the same. "Follow me."

She was surprised that he didn't call servants as he led her behind the throne. A small door was hidden in the wall and she discovered that the temple stretched a lot farther than she first thought. They walked through a narrow, dark hall in silence before stopping at a door. He opened it and stepped inside.

Water trickled over the edges of the rock like a waterfall, falling into a bathing pool. By the water's edge was everything she needed to wash and a fresh stack of clothes. She glanced at him, surprised. It was as if he'd been expecting her to come. Deciding that maybe he'd seen her coming up the stairs, she said nothing.

"Bathe, dress and I will come for you. Tonight the hall will be filled."

He was gone before she even turned around. Sonja sighed, glancing around to make sure she was alone. Slowly, she dropped her pack to the floor. The bath really did look tempting and it would be wrong to insult his generosity. She began to strip out of her clothes.

She felt strange, as if she could feel people all round her, but there were only the stone carvings of statues, much like the one in the jungle she'd struck with her knife.

Once undressed, she tested the water with her foot. It was warm and clear. It made her feel a little easier that she could see the bottom. Walking down the stairs beneath the surface, she moved to the side to grab the bar of soap. Sonja lathered her skin, pleased to find the soap was sweet smelling. She cleaned her large breasts, spending a little longer than normal on the sensitive globes as she thought of Pacal.

She knew it was wrong, but she found him oddly attractive—even if he was hidden behind a mask. There was a swarthy power and confidence to him. It was in the graceful way he moved and talked. He was well built and, from what she could see, really did have the body of an intergalactic bodybuilder champion. He'd probably be ugly as sin when he removed his mask, but she could imagine him any way she wanted.

Sonja took a deep breath, trying to bury the desire she felt. Now was not the time to give in to her arousal. She scrubbed her breasts harder, absently pinching her nipples as she tried really hard to ignore the ache between her thighs. Good thing her pussy was under water, so the cream that built there could be washed away.

It'd been a long time since she'd been with a man, perhaps too long. Her hands ran up over her neck into her hair, lathering the locks with the soap. A light moan escaped her.

Blessed Stars! She was horny.

When she closed her eyes, she imagined the masked stranger next to her, his poncho pulled up, as he fucked her in his ceremonial garb—mask and all. It was wicked and tempting at the same time. Her body jerked, her pussy flooded with moisture that had nothing to do with the bathing pool. She knew she should stop, knew that it wasn't in her best interest to stir her arousal.

Sonja moaned softly. Ah, to hell with her best interests. This fantasy was too good to pass up.

* * * * *

Pacal watched the woman from the narrow slit above the bathing chamber. There were several slits along the ceiling, from a time when the men would come to watch the women bathe, stroking their cocks to release. There'd been no women in the bathing pool for a long time, not until Sonja.

The woman was right below him, in the bath. He'd seen her glance around before grabbing the soap. She couldn't see him. From the bathing pool the eye slit looked like part of the carved design in the ceiling.

He watched her soap her large breasts, wondering what she thought about as she paid them extra attention. Swallowing, he suppressed a groan of appreciation. The woman was beautiful, with breasts so round and full he wanted to take his cock to them and feel their softness enclosing his thick shaft until he came, making a necklace with his seed around her throat.

His cock stirred, growing hard. Pacal angled its head, but it was hard to get a clear view with his mask on. Still, he tried, crawling along the floor to a new slit as she walked around in the bath. She washed her hair, rinsing it beneath the surface. When she moved to the stairs, he sighed in disappointment, thinking the show would be over. It had been many moons since he saw a naked woman.

Then, to his surprise, she sat on the steps, spreading her legs beneath the water. She leaned back in the pool, touching those glorious mounds of flesh, caressing her hands down her stomach. Pacal tensed, instantly reaching for his erection beneath the robes. He felt no remorse as he spied on her.

She dipped her fingers into her slit at the same moment he fisted his cock. He watched her stroke as she wantonly pleased herself. He moved his fist, keeping time with her rhythm, imagining what it would be like to fuck her, to have her tied down on an altar before him in an ancient ceremony.

Sonja pinched her nipples, letting loose a soft cry. Her back arched. She tensed as her beautiful body was brought to orgasm. The sight was too much. Pacal came hard, spilling his seed on the stone floor. His heart beat frantically in his chest and he rolled onto his back. It had been too long since he'd found release.

Chapter Two

The poncho Pacal had left for her was much like his — only much less material. The white cotton clung to her breasts, running down her front and back. Though it technically covered her private areas, a wide strip of flesh was left bare on both sides. The neckline dipped low, showing an indecent amount of cleavage. She was glad she had the breasts to carry the look off. A belt of gold fitted over her hips, dipping low at the front, keeping the gown from falling open at the sides.

Looking herself over, she couldn't help but feel seductive and sexy. It was more erotic than lingerie back home. There was also something to be said for not wearing underwear. She rolled her dirty clothes into a ball and shoved them into her pack. She'd worry about washing them later.

"You appear more relaxed. Did you enjoy yourself?"

Sonja tensed. She didn't hear Pacal approach but he stood right behind her. Getting quickly to her feet, she tried not to blush. Did he mean to ask if she felt better from taking a bath? Or did he know she'd pleasured herself? Almost as soon as she climaxed, she'd berated herself for being stupid. She didn't know what kind of technology these people had. Sure, they looked primitive, but the whole place could've been wired with cameras. That's all she needed — a tape of her masturbating floating around a primitive world.

Choosing to play ignorance, she said, "Yes, thank you for your hospitality. The bath was most welcome."

It was impossible to read his expressions beneath the turquoise mask and she suddenly hated not being able to see his face. Her fantasy came back to haunt her, as she knew it would.

She'd pictured him fucking her against the stairs as she touched herself—her body held down against stone as Pacal fucked her.

Cream moistened her pussy anew and, as he turned to lead her from the bathing room, she rubbed her thighs together in irritation to keep her juices from dripping down her legs. Sonja took a deep, calming breath. She had to get back on track.

Focus on the mission. That's what's important. Damn, he has a nice ass.

"Are you not curious as to my message?"

"Everything reveals itself in due time," he answered enigmatically. Torches lit the way from their places on the wall, casting him with orange light. "I imagine that will as well."

Well, he might not be curious as to what it said, but she sure as hell was. Just her luck, he'd probably not even tell her what was on it. She'd die an old maid, rocking in her chair, driving herself insane, never knowing.

"You said everyone would be coming tonight? Where are they? Hunting?" she asked, trying to make conversation.

"No," his voice so soft and sad that she barely heard it. "They don't hunt, not anymore. They don't do much of anything anymore. Besides, I said tonight the hall would be filled. I didn't say everyone was coming. Everyone is already here."

"Oh!" She was tempted to make a face at him but refrained from being childish. Her luck he'd actually have eyes on the back of his head and would see her.

She tried to concentrate, thinking of anything but how his hips moved as he walked, how she wanted to bend him over and give him a spanking on that firm ass.

Argh! Think of something else.

Sonja closed her eyes. Maybe everyone was below in the base of the strange temple pyramid.

"You must be hungry," he said, interrupting her thoughts. "Would you like to dine?"

"Yes, please." As if on cue, her stomach growled. She followed him, doing her best not to stare at his long, black hair as it brushed his delectable ass. It was hard though, as there was nothing else to look at in the narrow hall.

He led her around what had to be the wall behind his throne. Then, as they came to the end, the passageway opened up into a large room. A wooden table was in the middle, as fine as any she'd ever seen. It was laden with food and plates were set at two places near the head.

Pacal took a seat at the head of the table, motioning her to his side. She sat on a low chair. He sat above her, his chair higher than hers. Reaching forward, he began placing food on his plate. She watched him, expecting him to remove the mask. He didn't. Instead, he tilted the chin and ate small bites beneath it.

"You do not eat?" he asked.

Instead of answering, Sonja reached forward and placed bread and meat on her plate. They ate in silence, taking small bites. Goblets of wine were set before them and she took a sip. She looked for servants, anyone to have set the table. There was no one. They were alone.

Sonja wondered if she should try to make conversation. Would he be insulted? He hadn't seemed to be so far. Finally she decided that if she shouldn't, the A-mac would've warned her to be quiet.

"Do you leave here often?" she asked.

"No," he said. "I've not traveled down the stairs for many years."

"You don't get tired of being up here?"

"It doesn't matter what I tire of. Things are the way they are. I don't leave. That's the way of it." Pacal took a sip, working easily around his mask as if he'd eaten with it on many times. Curious, she wanted to rip it from his features, but refrained. Maybe it was better she didn't see his face. There might be a really good reason as to why it was hidden.

"So, you can't do what you want? Are you a prisoner?" she asked, intrigued. Oddly, she could really detect what he was feeling. She'd always been a little empathetic, but never this much. There was a sadness to him, but also an acceptance. When he moved, he was patient, relaxed, almost to the point of being resigned.

"We are all prisoners to our natures," he said. "The rest can't be helped. Fate decides what it will do with us. All we can do is accept it."

Sonja took a drink and leaned back, studying him. He turned to her, watching her just as intently. The air seemed to spark between them. She was hot, her stomach already aching to be filled.

Was this some kind of foreplay? A seduction? If so, Sonja wasn't protesting.

"I don't give you the answers you seek," he said.

"I don't seek anything," Sonja said, remembering why she was there. "My mission is to give you a missive. You have yet to give me permission to give you the missive and so I wait for that permission."

"And what will you do once I give you permission?"

"I'll give you the missive," she answered smiling.

"After that?"

"It depends on many factors." Sonja didn't want to admit that she didn't know.

"What do you wish to happen?"

"Hopefully, you'll agree to what it says and I'll be on my way."

"And where will you go?" His eyes stayed on her. They were dark, penetrating.

Sonja swallowed. Truth was, she didn't know that either.

"I see," he said, standing. "Come, they fill the hall. We should go."

Sonja stood, looking down at her outfit. Her heart beat nervously. Without thought, she blurted, "Am I to be sacrificed?"

He stopped walking and glanced at her. His eyes narrowed beneath the mask.

"I mean...this outfit. Is it...ahh...ceremonial in purpose?" she asked, thinking that Simon might have sent her here to be some kind of primitive sacrifice. Sonja never saw him to be that kind of man, but still, this was a strange assignment.

"No, I don't mean to kill you." Pacal walked out the door, pausing in the entryway to wait for her.

Sonja felt somewhat relieved by his admission. Though she wasn't sure if he could be trusted. She wanted to trust him, but her training as an RLS-69 taught her to trust no one.

Pacal led her back down the hall. She expected to go to the throne room to meet whoever it was he expected to come. Instead, he stopped and led her into a bedroom. There was a large bed with low tables placed around it. A large circular pit of fire gave the temple room light.

"You may stay here tonight." He glanced at her. "With me."

"Ah, wait," she said, unsure of the planet's protocol on refusing to share bedchambers with someone. She saw her backpack was on the floor, next to the bed. She tried to remember where she'd left it and couldn't. "I think you might have the wrong impression of why I came."

"I have no impression. You have not told me why you've come, beyond a missive you wish to give me." Pacal moved toward the bed, pulling off his belt and laying it over a low table next to it. Then he pulled off the headdress and set it down. Lightly, he shook his head, the long hair moving in waves over his body now that they were free.

His slow striptease made her mind fog for a moment. She licked her lips, waiting for him to pull his poncho up so she could finally see his firm body. Shaking her head, she came to her senses. She didn't move further into the room. Instead, she edged backward. "What about the hall? Don't you have guests?"

"They always come. We must not disturb them," he said. "Leave them to the hall. There they will stay until morning."

Sonja felt her body jolt with anticipation as she looked at the large bed and then to him. She waited to see if he'd take off the mask. He didn't. Pulling back a thick white blanket, Pacal lay down. She knew it should be some form of comfort that he remained clothed, but she felt oddly disappointed.

"I can only take that which is offered, if you are worried," he said. By the tone of his voice, she imagined he smiled at her, but with the mask there was no way to be sure.

"No." She blushed. "I wasn't worried. I was just...ah... thinking."

Sonja moved toward the bed, pulled back the covers and lay down. This was all too weird, but something deep inside her compelled her to do it. She knew her mission was to get him to agree to her missive by any means necessary. All RLS agents were given shots to prevent against diseases and pregnancy. She hadn't gotten one before leaving, but Abbi was thorough and would've told her if she needed them. So there was no reason not to see what would happen when she lay next to Pacal. If he tried anything weird, she knew how to defend herself.

The fire dimmed in brightness and she sat up, expecting to see someone tending it. There was no one there. Pacal stayed on the bed, unmoving. His chest rose in even sleep. She turned her back on him and closed her eyes.

This definitely had to be the strangest day ever.

* * * * *

Sonja awoke in the night with a jolt of surprise. A light sheen of sweat covered her skin, sticking her gown to her body. The two strips of the skirt tangled in her legs.

She breathed heavily, her body stirred with hot desire, every inch of her aching to be touched. It was like a fiery, passionate, yearning need that singed every pore, flooded every limb. Her nipples were hard peaks and her pussy dripped with cream, wetter than should've been possible.

Pacal had been in her dreams, making love to her. She glanced over at him, peeking at him under the pretense of sleeping. He hadn't moved. In fact, he'd been the perfect gentleman, not once touching her.

Too bad. She would've preferred to have him touching her. Just thinking of her dream made her nipples sting, shooting a trail of lust straight down to her already oversensitive cunt.

What was it he had said? *I can only take that which is offered, if you are worried.*

Was he waiting for her to offer herself to him? Dare she offer? Maybe she should test him. With a light moan, she pretended to toss in her sleep, moving her leg to touch his. His skin was warm. He didn't move.

So much for subtle.

She waited what seemed to be an appropriate amount of time before moving closer. Tossing her hand on his chest, she snuggled closer as if seeking warmth. Fire shot through every place their bodies touched. Her pussy was drenched, practically throbbing with need.

This is torture! Come on, Pacal, move.

"Are you trying to offer?" he asked, his voice calm as if he'd been lying awake the whole time, knowing what she was doing.

"Hmm?" she mumbled, still trying to cling to her cover story of being asleep. His chest quaked as if he laughed. Finally, she gave up and asked, "Haven't you ever heard of letting a woman have her dignity?"

"So you are offering?"

At least his chest stopped moving in laughter. That was something. Sonja sighed. "I don't know. Maybe."

"I can only take that which is offered. Until you're ready to ask me, please stop touching me," Pacal said. He didn't move.

Sonja started to draw away from him. It wasn't easy saying the words aloud. Once spoken, they couldn't be taken back. They made her desire for him all the more real. It made it impossible to blame her action on sleepiness, or dreams, or…or anything. If she said it, it would make it her desire, her will, her doing.

"Pacal?" she asked, nervous. She kept her hand on his chest. There was something about him, a connection she felt all the way to her core. It'd been there since the first moment she laid eyes on him.

"Yes?" The word was soft, low.

"Do you want me…" she hesitated. Closing her eyes, she managed, "… to offer?"

"You must ask?" He sounded surprised by this.

"Well, I mean, I don't know you. You wear that mask and—"

"I won't take it off," he said instantly, stiffening beneath her palm.

"Oh, no, I wouldn't ask you to." He relaxed. She meant it, in a way. She did want to see his face, but part of the eroticism was not seeing his face. "It's just that, well, I can't see your expressions so I don't…"

"Offer if you wish to offer, then you will have my answer," he said, still not touching her. Was it her imagination, or did his breath catch?

"Pacal, will you make love to me?"

He finally moved, rolling onto his side to face her. "You ask for this?"

"Yes," she said, nodding. Her breath caught. She kept her hand on his chest. They were close. She looked into his eyes, trying to see him through the mask he wore. He smelled really good, like a man should smell—potent, virile, seductive.

"You ask for love, not sex?" he insisted.

"Well, making love," Sonja didn't know what else to say to that. Saying "fuck me" seemed a little harsh, even if that's what she wanted him to do. "Isn't it the same thing?"

"Perhaps," he agreed, before adding, "Yes, I'll make love with you."

His jaw tilted down, as he moved his hand beneath her arm to the naked side of her breast. With a gentle sweep of his fingers, he drew his hand down her side to her hip. He moved over the belt, leaving it intact, before drawing his hand around to the bottom curve of her ass cheek.

Sonja's mouth opened as she gasped for breath. It had been so long since she'd been touched. His warm, rough palms kneaded her flesh, heating her already hot body. She leaned in to him, wanting to kiss him. Running her hand over his arm, she pulled him closer. A soft moan left her as she felt the hard outline of his cock pressing against her stomach. She leaned forward, kissing his neck. He stiffened at the contact.

"Must you wear this robe?" she asked, kissing him again, letting the tip of her tongue flicker over his delicious flesh. Sonja tugged the poncho up, working it with her fingers as she exposed his thighs. "Or is this like the mask, staying put regardless?"

"No," he chuckled. Pacal sat up, pulling the garment over his head.

Sonja watched his body in the soft firelight. He was gorgeous. Black tattoos wrapped around his biceps, matching a pair of bands around his upper thighs. She touched his leg, finding the tattooed flesh as smooth as the rest of him. His cock stood tall, a veritable weapon in its size as it reached up from his muscled body. Leaning over, she kissed his thigh. "Did these hurt?"

"My marks?" he asked, sounding distracted. "No."

She kissed him again, flicking her tongue against his hot flesh.

"That feels…"

"Good?" she supplied.

"Yes, but I was going to say strange," Pacal admitted.

Sonja was surprised by that. "Don't you kiss?"

"Kiss?"

"Like this." Sonja ran her hands over his hips, kissing him fully with her opened mouth. She liked the clean taste of him, as she moved her lips up over his naked thighs.

"No, we…my culture…we don't use our mouths." He tensed each time her mouth pressed to him.

Sonja grinned. That was just way too much temptation. He really didn't know what he was missing. She crawled up over him, nestling her legs between his. She spread his legs apart, rubbing his chest with her palms. "Mm, tell me. How do your people make love?"

"We touch," he said. She leaned over to kiss his nipple. He tensed, not moving until she stopped. "Then we…" She flicked her tongue over his other nipple, wetting it. Again he didn't speak until she drew away. "…we, ah, join."

"Mm, so you've never been kissed before?" she asked, not really paying attention to her words as she ran her tongue down his stomach. Not an ounce of fat marred his perfect frame. Rimming his navel, she felt him jerk, his muscles going stiff.

"Ah." Pacal writhed beneath her. His hands glided over her flesh, but he didn't do more than touch her lightly. "No."

"Then allow me to pleasure you," Sonja whispered, feeling empowered.

"You are already pleasing me." Moving to sit up, he reached for her, but she pushed him in the center of his chest, knocking him down.

"You haven't felt anything yet."

Sonja determined to make this an experience he never forgot. She liked knowing she could teach him something new, that she'd be the first to take his cock between her lips. Kissing down his stomach, she settled herself between his legs. His cock was thick, long, and her mouth watered to be so close to it.

She ran her hands over his stomach, massaging down his thighs, between his legs, moving to cup his balls. He groaned, loud and long, as she fondled them. Sonja licked the tip of his penis, already tasting pre-come on it. Progressing slowly, she licked her way down one side, kissing and nibbling as she went. Then, working her way around the base, she nibbled and licked her way back up to the tip.

He clenched the mattress. She moaned softly to let him know she enjoyed herself. Rolling her tongue, she sucked the blunted tip between her lips. Pacal lurched up on the bed. She pulled off, giving him a look of warning as she pushed him back down.

"Just let me do this," she urged.

"I would not stop you," he admitted, hoarse. "Please, continue."

Sonja giggled, sucking him again between her lips. Animalistic noises left them, primal and raw as she moved. She rolled her tongue along the ridge she found on his cock head. Then, sucking harder, she took it halfway into her mouth, pumping her lips up and down, up and down. She scraped her teeth along the smooth shaft, trying to deep-throat him. He was too big. Using her hand, she stroked his extra length.

Sweat beaded his flesh and she felt him holding back. It only made her suck harder. Her hand found his balls, squeezing and rolling, as a finger slipped behind them to the cleft of his ass. Finding the sensitive flesh she knew to be there, she probed gently. His sac tightened and he bucked off the bed, coming in a long, tasty stream into her mouth.

He shook violently, with a half grunt, half growl. When she'd sucked him dry, she leaned back, provocatively licking her lips. He was breathing heavily, shaking.

"I take it you like kissing?" she teased.

"I have never felt anything like it."

"You know, men can kiss women as well."

He tensed. "I can't take off my mask."

"I wouldn't ask you to. I was just letting you know for future reference. That if you ever wanted, you could kiss me..." Sonja ran her hands down her body, brushing her garment aside so she could touch her wet pussy. She didn't mind the mask, even if it did look daunting in the firelight. She stroked her clit, parting her wet folds. "...right here."

"You have showed me your way."

"One of them," she put forth, grinning.

"Let me give you pleasure in mine." Pacal sat up. "Undress."

Sonja looked down, surprised to see he was fully erect, almost appearing larger than the time before. She pulled off the belt, easily sliding her gown over her head. Unable to stop herself, she touched her breasts, massaging the large globes in her palms. It felt wonderful and she moaned.

"Keep touching yourself if it gives you pleasure," he said. He got off the bed and crossed naked to a low dresser. He took out a bundle and carried it back with him. Sonja eyed it, curious. Pacal took up his belt and threaded it through a loop in the wall, above her head. "Come here."

Sonja hesitated.

"Come here," he repeated, holding his hand to her. "I trusted you for your way. You will enjoy this."

How could she refuse? She moved forward, facing the wall at his urging. She let him tie her wrists so they were trapped close to the wall, but allowing enough room for her hands to brace her weight on the bed. He shifted the bed behind her. She glanced over her shoulder to watch as he unwrapped the bundle. Her thighs were slick with desire and she knew if he didn't claim her soon she'd die from lust.

To her fascination, and trepidation, he took a large dildo from the cloth and strapped it about his firm waist. Sonja struggled against her binds, pulling to be free. They were secure.

Taking a small container, he dipped his fingers inside and lathered the cream on both his hard cock and the large dildo strapped above it.

"That second one really isn't necessary," she said, shaking.

Pacal only laughed. She knew what he planned, knew that it was physically possible to be double stuffed, but she'd never had it done to her. Hell, she'd only tried anal sex once before. Though she'd enjoyed it, it had been a tight squeeze.

Despite her fears, her pussy let loose a large torrent of cream. He came up behind her, reaching around to pinch her nipples. Her back arched in response.

"I like the largeness of your breasts," he said. She felt his mask brushing up against her shoulder. "They flow out of my hands."

Pacal continued to touch her, stroking her stomach, her thighs, rubbing the slick pearl buried in her tender folds. With deft precision, he thumped her clit, jolting her entire body with sensations, and his finger drummed a primal beat along the swollen bud. She writhed before him, tugging at her binds. Then he pinched her aching clit, rolling it around until she forgot all about his plans to fuck her with two at once.

"There are many things I would like to do to you," he admitted. When he drew up, she felt the brush of two blunted tips caressing the back of her thigh. She remembered the thick strap-on set over his even thicker cock.

She expected him to take her body's entrances one at a time, easing her body to what he planned, and was surprised when she felt both his cock and his strap-on probing her at once. The cream he slathered himself with eased the penetration. He thrust up, moving slowly as he broke open her ass and pussy at the same time.

Sonja cried out, feeling very full. It had been so long since she'd been fucked and now she was getting more than she'd ever bargained for. He pinched her nipples hard, keeping his fingers clamped on the sensitive tips. She convulsed, pushing him deeper without meaning to.

"Ah, yes," he growled along her neck. "That's it. You're easing up. Break yourself open on me. Keep taking them in until you get it all."

Sonja was far from being virginal, but that's how she felt. Never had she had a cock so big—in either hole. The pressure felt good and she couldn't help but push back for more. The dildo was firm, yet rubbery, as it parted her ass cheeks wide. When she felt herself getting close, he thrust, seating himself to the hilt.

Sonja gasped in delight, becoming mindless. Pulling against her restraints, she moved on him, taking shallow thrusts at first as she got used to his size. Pacal let her fuck him, let her set the pace, as he tweaked her nipples.

Only after her body had eased to accept what he was doing did he pump his hips. It felt so good, even as she felt like she was being ripped apart. She tensed, coming swiftly to a tremulous release.

Pacal groaned, releasing his seed inside her body. The cool mask bumped her shoulder, scraping her skin with its rougher surface, as he laid his forehead along her neck. Instantly, he reached to release her hands, pulling the cocks from her body. Sonja fell to the bed in a weak and trembling mass.

Okay, his way is better than mine.

Chapter Three

Sonja had no problem sleeping after being so thoroughly fucked by Pacal. The next morning, when she awoke, she was alone in his room. It was still dim, the fire the only light. Her body twitched in protest as she tried to move. Grinning with the memory, she knew she'd probably be walking funny this morning. Her gut twinged.

Correction. I'll be walking funny for at least a week. Bless you, Simon, Pacal more than makes up for the bugs.

Fresh clothes were laid out on the end of the bed, next to a tray of food. She took a bite of the fresh fruit as she dressed. Her outfit this morning was the same as the night before, only there was a jacket-like robe to go over the gown. The jacket covered her sides from view. After breakfast, she went to her pack. The letter was still there. She picked it up and slid it into her gown, using the belt to keep it secure against her hip.

It wasn't too hard to find her way to the main stone chamber. She expected to find some remnants of a party the night before. There was nothing. Pacal wasn't even there. Walking outside, she looked for him. The blue Grafowk was perched outside. She began to stretch when it flew and landed on her forearm.

"Why hello, friend," she said, giggling in surprise. "I'm sorry. I don't have any food today."

The bird didn't seem to mind. He walked his way up her arm to perch on her shoulder. She walked over the platform outside, refusing to go down the long row of steps. If she went down, she'd only have to walk back up and her body was too sore from Pacal's penetrating touch to make the trip.

She moved around the pyramid, looking down over the abandoned village. There weren't signs of anyone, just abandoned buildings, statues and carvings.

"He's taken to you."

Sonja turned, almost feeling shy. Pacal was behind her. She wished she could see his face to know if he smiled at her.

"I was looking for you," she admitted.

"Were you? I was with the others. I told them of your visit." Pacal looked at the bird. He again wore the headdress. The bird squawked and flew away.

"You did?" Sonja blushed. "What did you say?"

"That you have come with a message," he said. "And that you offered to make love to me."

"Oh." Sonja wanted to throw herself off the side of the temple. He said it so matter-of-fact.

"They were happy."

Great. They're happy you're getting laid.

"Oh," she said again, unable to think of anything better.

"Are you hungry? They have brought food." Pacal reached his hand as if to touch her. He held back, hand suspended in air.

"They're waiting? Inside?"

Oh, how embarrassing!

Hi, everyone, I'm the slut who slept with your temple guy on the first night. How ya doin'?

"Yes, they are always inside," he said. "Only I come out."

"Am I to meet them?"

"No, but perhaps someday."

Sonja didn't take his hand. She wondered if he was a little crazy. Maybe he'd been isolated for so long he was seeing imaginary people. Her stomach knotted.

Okay, the more she thought about it, the more she began to think that maybe he was crazy. He did wear a mask around all the time and never left the temple. Maybe he killed everyone and their dead bodies were stuffed like dolls, which he moved around and talked to. The place did look abandoned and she'd yet to hear anyone.

When she looked at him, she didn't get that sicko vibe off him. But, well, her RLS-69 training did say she was going to be dealing with dangerous life and death situations. She should be very careful with this one.

"No," she said answering his earlier question. "I'm not hungry. I ate the tray of fruit in your room."

"There was a tray?" he asked, tilting his head to the side.

"Yes," she answered, "along with this gown. Was I not supposed to take it?"

"No, if it was there, it was for you," he said. "They must have left it."

Again with the "they".

"I'd like to thank them."

"I'll let them know," he answered, nodding.

"Yeah, all right, you do that, Pacal."

"What's wrong? You look at me strangely today. Did you not enjoy last night? Did I not please you?"

Last night the mask didn't bother her, but right now, she really wanted to see his face, read his expression. He sounded kind, hopeful, gentle even. But not being able to see a smile…

She frowned, hating his turquoise mask. It didn't really matter what he looked like. She wasn't shallow, not very shallow anyway.

"Did I not please you?" he asked, his tone softer, insistent, maybe even worried.

She took a deep breath. She really wanted to lie to him, but oddly, she couldn't do it. "Yes, you pleased me very much."

"So you frown?"

"Are you frowning?" she returned. "You see, because I can't tell."

"My mask," he stated, his tone flat.

"It's really not necessary, is it? Do you wear it for religious purposes? Do your beliefs dictate that you sleep and eat in it?" she asked, placing her hands on her hips. "How much would you like it if you couldn't see my face?"

To her surprise, he admitted, "Not at all. I wouldn't like it. I like seeing your face."

"I have a missive for you, Pacal," she stated.

"I know."

She took it out of the folds of her gown. "Give me permission to give it to you."

"You look beautiful in the sunlight. I like your hair. It's very pretty. Such a brilliant, rich red."

Sonja dropped her arm. "Pacal—"

He stepped closer, cutting off her protest as he moved his fingers to touch her hair, pulling the long strands as he stroked her. "I wish to take your offer again."

Sonja's mouth worked but no sound came out. He pulled her body close. His arousal pressed into her stomach. A weak moan escaped her, until all she saw and felt was him.

Unable to stop herself, she wrapped her arms around his neck. The letter fell from her fingers. She gasped, but the Grafowk swept from the sky and grabbed it. The bird looked at her before flying away.

Pacal's mask nuzzled her throat. She didn't care about the letter—not right at this moment. Turning slightly, she ran her hands over his body, feeling his muscles beneath his clothes. Sonja couldn't stop. She needed to feel him, wanted him inside her.

The jungle spread out below them. The sun was bright and warm. He pushed her dress aside and pulled up her gown. Her legs were bared to him. Sonja was just as eager, pulling up his poncho to free his stiff cock. Her pussy was wet, ready to be claimed.

Pacal lifted her, squeezing her ass, as he pressed her to the outside wall of the temple. He thrust up, prying her body open. She was still a little sore from the night before, but her body welcomed him. The mask buried in her throat, oddly cool as her legs dangled behind him. Her back pressed into unforgiving stone. Primal sounds escaped their lips.

Pacal pumped into her, riding her in firm strokes. It felt so good. Sonja cried out in pleasure, urging him on. "Oh, yes, Pacal, yes, fuck me. Ah, right there, don't stop. That feels so good."

At her words, he thrust harder, pounding at her core. It was erotic, watching the sunlight on the jungle behind him, his glorious body taking her up against the temple wall, his long dark hair crashing around her, pushed to her by the breeze.

At the same time, she knew it was crazy. She was fucking a stranger she didn't know anything about. Sure, she'd been taught seduction, but this was her first mission and the RLS training didn't say anything about meeting a man like Pacal. And to make matters worse, she thought she might have feelings for him. No. She couldn't love him. That was crazy, almost as crazy as he was. But the feelings were there, building inside her like the sexual tension his cock wrought on her pussy.

"Pacal," she breathed, unable to fight her heart. It was too much. It felt too good, too right. "Pacal."

The orgasm hit her hard, racking her body in violent tremor. He grunted, coming inside her, filling her womb with his hot seed. She whimpered softly, holding the side of his mask, wanting to rip it off him.

"Pacal," she said, her words breathless. "What's happening?"

"I'm making love to you." He let her legs slide down his body so she could again support herself.

"I lost the letter," she whispered.

"It will be returned." He took her hand, leading her to the front entryway. "Come with me. I wish to take your offering again."

* * * * *

Pacal was pleased, though that happiness scared him. Sonja was so sweet, so giving a lover. When he was buried inside her, he never wanted to leave.

He crossed the hall, wondering if she was truly the one, the one the prophecy foretold. Was the period of darkness finally to end? He'd given up long ago that the prophecy was true, but what if he'd been wrong?

The urge to take her was strong in him. He wanted to fuck her, make love to her softly. He wanted to take her again and again, until she was bathed in his seed, until her belly was swollen with the life he had helped to create. When she'd taken him in her mouth, he'd been surprised. Never had he dreamt such a thing would bring him pleasure.

He was so lost in thoughts of what he wanted to do to her that when he felt Sonja's hand on his ass, he was surprised. He stopped before his throne in the ceremonial hall and turned. Instantly, she pressed her body to his.

"Right here is good," she whispered. "I want you here."

His cock lurched to full attention, more than ready to comply with her body's demands. She walked aggressively to him, pushing his chest to move him back toward his throne.

"Take a seat," she ordered.

Pacal instantly sat. He liked her games, her adventurous spirit. He'd sensed it in her that first moment, when the Grafowk let her touch it.

Sonja ran her hands up his thighs, kneeling before him. He touched her face, liking the softness of her skin. She worked his poncho up over his thighs, freeing his cock to view. He tensed, seeing the look on her face, the way she licked her mouth. He knew what she was doing even before she lowered her mouth to suck his shaft between her lips.

Glorious heat shot down his cock, shooting pleasure down to his balls and up throughout his body. Pacal pushed his hands into her hair, arching his hips as he pumped himself into her warm mouth. He didn't want it to stop.

He felt a presence around them and quickly pulled her off before she'd finished. She looked dazed, her lids lazily dipping over her eyes. Instantly, she moved onto his lap, straddling him on his throne. He knew he should protest, but couldn't form the words as she bared her thighs and brought her wet, hot pussy over him. She thrust down, sheathing him completely, her body more than ready to accept him.

Her legs dangled over the sides of the throne. Pacal groaned, grabbing her hips. He moved her up and down, not caring that they were being watched. More gathered in the hall.

He tore her gown, freeing her large breasts. Pinching her nipples, he rejoiced as she cried out. Cream poured out of her, making his cock glide. Suddenly, she arched, her body clamping down on him hard. He couldn't hold back, as he released himself into her.

Afterwards, she lay weakly against his shoulder. "I'm falling in love with you."

"I know," he answered, his chest tightening. "I know."

I know.

Sonja pushed up, climbing off his lap. That's all he had for her? She confessed her heart and all he said was "I know"?

A tingle worked over her spine and she quickly turned. The hall was empty.

"They are pleased you're here," Pacal said.

"They?" she whispered. There was no one there. They were alone in the hall.

"Yes, they've come to see you."

"Oh." Sonja fought back tears. It was as she feared. He was crazy. She licked her lips. "I have to…ah…get something from my bag. I'll be right back."

"Sonja?"

"Just a moment."

Sonja didn't know what she was doing, but she knew she had to go. She couldn't survive in the jungle without supplies and she definitely couldn't stay in the crazy man's temple any longer. Running to his room, she found her pack on the floor. She didn't bother to change out of the dress. Putting her hiking boots on, she slid the pack on her shoulders.

A chill went up her spine as she stood. Spinning on her heels, she looked around. No one was there. Her eyes met with a statue. She'd seen them all over the temple, strange, square-bodied things, so muscular that the gods would have been envious of them.

"You're just edgy, that's all," she whispered to herself. Licking her lips, she looked out into the hall. It was empty. She made her way down the narrow hall for the front entrance.

"You're wrong," Pacal's voice said.

There was no answer.

"No, stop saying that. You're wrong," he insisted. "She won't leave."

Like hell, I won't.

Sonja edged in the dark shadows of the wall, trying to creep to the entrance without him seeing her. She could only hope that his craziness would trap him in the temple and she'd be able to get free. Pacal said he couldn't leave the temple and that he didn't go down the stairs.

The bird had taken her letter, so it wasn't like she could finish her mission. It wasn't her fault he refused to ask her for it. Seeing freedom, she ran.

"Sonja?" Pacal called behind her. "Sonja, wait!"

She heard footsteps and knew he chased her. A squeal left her lips as she ran for the door. Bright sunlight greeted her and she blinked as the Grafowk flew past her face, squawking. She screamed but forged onward, terrified.

"Sonja!" Pacal cried. "Sonja, no, wait!"

She reached the steps, taking them two and three at a time.

"Sonja, wait, come back!"

"Sonja!" Pacal's heart beat furiously in his chest. He saw her reach the first step, a point he couldn't cross. He tried anyway, knowing he couldn't go down. A force stopped him, hitting him in the face like a brick wall.

"Sonja, please, wait!"

Behind him his people gathered. He heard them talking, murmuring to themselves. He couldn't see them, but he heard them, felt them.

"Sonja," he said softly. He fell to his knees.

Suddenly, she stopped and looked at him. He lifted his hand, but he could only reach so far before he was blocked. He hit the field, wanting to follow her, but couldn't make it move. In over five hundred years he'd never been able to make it move.

His heart nearly stopped beating as she took a slow step back up. Hope tried to build. His people quieted behind him, waiting, as anxious as he.

"What's going on here, Pacal?" she asked, cautious. "I want you to tell me what's wrong with you."

"Sonja—"

"Are you crazy?" She took another step. Then, to herself, she whispered, "Am I crazy for talking to you?"

He ran his hand over the invisible barrier that kept him from being able to go after her. Sonja reached out and he knew she was trying to feel the barrier. Her hand fell through air and she couldn't. Pacal reached for her, but she pulled away too quickly.

The voices behind him began to argue. He turned, yelling, "Quiet!"

They instantly obeyed.

"Pacal? Who are you talking to? There's no one there."

"You just can't see them," he whispered. "Trust me, they are there."

"No, there's no one there." She bit her lips. Tears came to her eyes. He wanted to comfort her but couldn't. "Tell me what's going on. Make me understand."

"I can't," he said. "I can't."

Death would come for all if he told. It was his burden to bear, his alone until…

"Yes, you can," Sonja said, trembling. She didn't know what was going on with him, but there had to be something. "You can trust me."

"I do trust you," he answered. The turquoise mask glinted in the sun. "It is you who doesn't trust me."

"How can I? I can't even see your face. I can't read your mind. It's like talking to a wall." Sonja began to turn, intent on walking away. She stopped, moving to face him once more. "Tell me why I can trust you. Tell me why I should."

"My…heart…" he said, softly. He looked as if he would say more, but the Grafowk flew in front of him, flapping his wings in anger. The letter was clutched in his talons. The bird dropped it on the ground before him. Pacal took it and held it up to her.

"That's yours."

His fingers shook as he slowly nodded his head. He slowly opened it. She couldn't read his expression through the mask.

"What does it say?" she asked.

"The same as all the others."

"Which is?"

"It is time to let you go," he said.

Pacal turned, his head down. He walked toward the inside of the temple. Sonja watched him. She was free. The message was delivered. She could go. He wasn't going to try and stop her. Her mission was done. If the letter said to let her go, he was. She couldn't understand why RLS-69 would send her on a stupid mission like this, but they had.

Chapter Four

Sonja couldn't do it. She couldn't force herself to leave, couldn't force herself to even turn away from the temple. Taking a deep breath, she climbed to the top of the stairs.

The Grafowk stared at her. She reached into her pack and tossed a piece of meat at the bird perched at the temple door. He caught it and as he was busy eating, she went inside.

Pacal sat at his throne, his head down. She felt his sadness, or maybe she imagined it. Sonja wasn't sure of anything anymore. Maybe she was as crazy as he was.

"I don't want to go," she said, her voice low. Pacal's head whipped up to stare at her. Forcing her words to be stronger, she said, "I don't want to leave."

"Why would you wish to stay here? I don't blame you for going. I would leave if I could."

"What traps you?" She knew before she said the words that he wouldn't tell her. "It doesn't matter. What I want to know is if you want me to stay."

"Yes."

"And do you love me, or do you at least think you'll come to love me in time?"

"Yes."

Sonja took a deep breath. She braved a step forward. "I don't know how. I don't know why, but I was sent here for a reason. I think that reason was you. I can see why you've gone mad, being isolated in this prison of yours. I don't know what's happening and I may never know. But I love you. So help me, I'm as crazy as you are, because I've fallen in love with you overnight. I can't explain it, but I feel as if I've known you my whole life, and yet I know nothing about you."

He said nothing, didn't move.

"Take off your mask, Pacal. I don't care what you look like. Take it off. Let me see your face." Sonja stopped before him. He didn't move.

"I can't remove the mask," was all he said.

"Then let me."

The Grafowk squawked behind her as she reached for him. He didn't move, letting her touch his mask. She tried to pull, but it was stuck. Digging her fingers around the edge, it felt as if it was adhered to his flesh. A weak sound of pain left him as she pulled hard.

Bright blue wings flapped in her face, knocking her back. Sonja fell to the floor. She watched as the bird grabbed Pacal's mask. Pacal screamed. The bird squawked. Sonja watched, helpless.

She heard excited murmurs all around them. But when she glanced around, there was no one there.

The Grafowk ripped off the mask, flying back with it. Sonja moved to see Pacal's face but was blinded by light. She lifted her hand to block it, closing her eyes tight. The whispering voices grew and then suddenly were silent.

"Sonja?"

Sonja was too afraid to look. She licked her lips, shaking.

"Sonja?" she heard Pacal say again. A warm hand touched her cheek, only to be replaced by warmer lips. She gasped, blinking in surprise. He pulled on her arm, helping her up.

She hesitated before looking at his face. She gasped. He was handsome. Beyond handsome. He was quite possibly the most gorgeous man she'd ever laid eyes on. He had dark, strong features and a firm mouth.

"Why would you hide?" she asked. "You're perfect."

He grinned. "No, you're perfect. You broke the curse that's haunted this temple for over five hundred years. Your ability to love unconditionally, without knowing or understanding. Your faith in your heart, in me. That is what's perfect."

"Pacal?" a shout sounded. The first was soon joined by others. Sonja watched as the hall filled with people—all caramel-skinned and dressed in outfits similar to Pacal's. They were smiling, cheering, chanting Pacal's name.

Sonja suddenly noticed that all the statues were gone. "What's happening? Where did all these people come from?"

"I told you, they were here the whole time. Their bodies were trapped in stone, but their spirits were trapped within the temple walls. Only I could hear them, but to speak this would have been to kill them."

"The whole time?" she asked, blushing as he turned to hide against his arm. "You mean, they saw…"

He laughed. She loved the sound of it. Pacal pulled her into his arms, holding her close. "Don't think about it. They couldn't have enjoyed it as much as I did."

How could she not think about it? Her blush deepened. She made a weak sound and hit his arm.

"You say I broke a curse?" she asked.

"I couldn't tell you before." Pacal took her hand and moved to his throne. He sat down, drawing her onto his lap. Sonja nestled against him, watching his handsome face as he spoke over the excited crowd. "Several of my people wanted to overthrow the gods. As punishment we were cursed. I had no part in it, but because I stood by their side and did nothing, I was cursed to walk alone, wearing this mask until the day my heart could be made whole."

"And the letter?"

"The same each time. As soon as I took it, it meant I had to let the bearer go." Pacal nuzzled her neck.

Sonja frowned, pulling back. "Hey, what do you mean every time? How many have come?"

"A hundred, perhaps. Why?"

"You've had a hundred women up here?" Sonja frowned.

"You're jealous of this?" he asked.

"Well, no, but..." Okay, she was jealous.

"There is no reason. I didn't love them. They didn't make love with me." Pacal nuzzled her throat, rubbing his skin along hers. "Mm, it's been so long since I've felt anything against my face but cold metal."

"So you didn't have sex with them?" Sonja ran her fingers through his long hair, touching him. The hall behind them began to clear as the excitement was taken outside. Still, they ignored the others.

"Well, yes, some," he answered honestly.

Sonja stiffened. "You just said they didn't make love to you."

"They didn't." Pacal laughed. "Only you asked to make love to me. They fucked me."

"That makes it so much better," she grumbled.

"You have no reason for this jealousy," he whispered. "You're who my heart has chosen. It if was not so, the curse wouldn't have been lifted."

Pacal stood, taking her hand.

"What happened to the mask?" she asked.

"The Grafowk has taken it back to the gods to let them know our punishment is over. He was my keeper and only he could decide to let me go. Until today, he's never come in here. And until you, none before had ever touched him."

"I think I understood more when I thought you were crazy," she said, laughing and so very happy. She wrapped her arms around his neck. "But I do love you."

"You'll be happy here?"

"Depends, can you leave the temple now?"

"Let us find out." Pacal grinned. She loved seeing his face. He pulled her toward the entrance. Sonja gasped. The city below them was full and more people were coming out of the jungle. "Come, I'll introduce you to my people."

Pacal started down the steps. A group of guards stopped them. Sonja frowned. One of the men looked very familiar. His leg was bleeding.

"Oh, no," she whispered.

"What is it?"

"I think I did that," she said, pointing at the man's leg. "I accidentally hit a statue with my knife."

"He'll live." Pacal started to move.

"Ah, actually, let's stay up here. I think you might have forgotten how long it takes to walk up and down these things."

"But—"

"Let's save it for tomorrow." She pulled him to her. "Right now I want to kiss you."

Pacal glanced down at his crotch. "Ah, you wish...to put your mouth on me? Right here?"

"Oh yeah." Sonja grinned. She lifted up on her toes and kissed him, rolling her tongue past his teeth. Pacal gasped in obvious surprise, giving her entrance as she kissed him. A soft moan left her and she felt his excitement pressing against her stomach. Suddenly, she noticed that everyone had stopped their cheering and talking.

Sonja pulled back. Everyone was staring at them, their eyes wide to see what she was doing to their leader.

Pacal moaned. "Yes, introductions can definitely wait until tomorrow."

Sonja giggled. He took her by the hand and rushed to get back inside. His people shouted in protest, obviously wanting a speech from him.

Pacal stopped, looked them over. "This is your new queen. We're going to bed."

Sonja gasped. "Pacal!"

"What, they've had me for over five hundred years. It's your turn to have me." Pacal lifted her into his strong arms. Carrying her inside, he licked at her mouth. "Besides, you said something about being able to kiss you as you kiss me."

He grinned with meaning, glancing down her body. Sonja squirmed, instantly moist.

"Maybe we better put off those introductions for a few days," she suggested. "I have a feeling we're going to be pretty busy."

"Mm, yes, we are going to be very busy. With the new child coming and all."

Sonja's brow furrowed. "There are children coming too?" She tried to look over his shoulder but his soft laugh stopped her.

"There haven't been children here in five hundred years."

"But you just said…"

Opening the door to his room, he walked her over to his bed. Sonya's eyes widened in anticipation as he spread her out before him. His hand went to her lower abdomen and he smiled down at her. "In nine golden moons we shall have the first child the temple has seen in centuries."

Sonja glanced down and the realization of what he was implying set in. "Oh, no. I'm not…we're not…how do you know?"

Pacal laughed and moved over her. "Yes, we are, and I would have thought you'd have learned to trust in me, even when you cannot see it with your own eyes."

She smiled and wrapped her legs around him. "Guess you should get started in the kissing department. I've heard that pregnant women are very horny."

Pacal looked shocked. "Your kind grows horns while the child is within you?"

Sonja giggled and pulled his smooth cheeks to her. Kissing his lips gently, she looked into he dark eyes. "Oh, I have so much to teach you."

"And I am very willing to learn."

Part Four
Trinity

Chapter One

"Simon, Abbi, do you read me?" Agent Trinity spoke into her wrist as the fuzzy effects of the A-mac rippled through her body. Looking around, she took in the sights of Mixlione and let a smile creep over her face. It'd been too long since she'd been on the party scene and this place looked as though it played host to a perma-party.

I can work with this.

Being locked away on Restigatio for the past two years had left her longing for some good times. It had been too long since she had a stiff drink and an even stiffer cock, preferably one not clothed under her boss' slacks.

Granted, Simon had her almost screaming out in ecstasy with the power he'd covered her with, but it felt wrong to have done that with him. He'd been one of her only friends for years. No part of her wanted to jeopardize that.

A girl could go only so long without sex before she either lost her mind or sprained her fingers from self-pleasuring. It wasn't as though the guards on Restigatio were anything that appealed to her. Since she was an RLS agent, many of them assumed they were able to not only date but fuck her as well. It was easy to see why the guards would assume that. Many of the agents did sleep with them. Some even had relationships that lasted only to the point that Simon found out about it.

Simon didn't go for relationships between guards and agents and the men knew it. But who could blame them? The agents were pretty, single, hot. And it wasn't like they really had to do guard duty. The agents roamed freely around the RLS facility so there was nothing really to guard. The only time they had to work was if anyone escaped. No one had ever escaped. Abbi made sure of that.

Still, if Trinity had really wanted to, she could've ridden several of them until she reached her zenith. After they served their base purpose in giving her pleasure, she would've cast them aside. But the idea of taking a man she didn't want turned her stomach.

Because of her pickiness, Trinity was left to either sleep with men on missions, which she didn't do, or masturbate. Needless to say, she picked the latter of the two and was now an expert at it. Yeah, she could make herself come in less than five minutes. As sad as that was, it beat letting strange men fondle her.

When Simon approached her about joining the elite rehabilitation unit of the RLS-69s, she'd jumped at the chance to get out of that hellhole commonly referred to as the general prison population. It wasn't every day that an inmate on Restigatio was afforded an opportunity to shorten their sentence—especially an inmate who'd been convicted of murder. She would've been a fool to pass it up.

Trinity was a lot of things, but a fool wasn't one of them.

Tapping the RL-com chip embedded in her wrist once, she waited for the tingling sensation that indicated it was activated. She had this happen before. The A-mac didn't get the information she needed implanted during her transfer down and she had to download it manually with the com chip.

She frowned. The com part didn't seem to be working. No one was answering her.

Though by the slight tingle in her head, she knew the information would be coming soon. Now, all Trinity had to do was stay hidden until the planet downloads took effect. If she were lucky, it'd happen any moment. Knowing her luck, it'd be an hour or better. She'd been on too many missions to expect this one to flow smoothly. They never did. If she wasn't being hunted by a serial killer, she was knee deep in Garifton's green swamps being attacked by giant killer leeches.

She shuddered at the thought of the sludge that she'd been forced to crouch down in as she watched a rebel base for the greater portion of a week. By the third day, she smelled as bad as the swamp and was sure the odor would never go away. Upon her return to RLS-69 headquarters, Abbi had promptly disinfected her.

Trinity looked around, nervous that her new assignment might involve a similar situation. Glancing down, she saw she was dressed in a slinky black dress, pantyhose and heels. Hopefully, the dress clothes meant no swamps. As comforting as that was, it still didn't rule out the prospect of serial killers.

Oh, well, a girl can't have everything.

It never ceased to amaze her how the A-mac knew exactly what to clothe them in while transporting them to their target destination. It even remembered to equip her with some of her favorite weapons, a phaser ring and heels with retractable blades in them. In a tight pinch, she could slice or blast her way out — always a fun tension reliever.

Trinity opened her black handbag and found it filled to the brim with odd colored chips. A square card held an image of her face and had writing on it she couldn't, as of yet, read. Once the planet files loaded, she'd know what it said.

One thing was for certain, her first name would remain the same. That was the only stipulation she had before doing each mission. Changing names constantly increased the chances of a slipup, and having her cover blown could leave her dead. Death wasn't exactly high on her list of lifelong dreams, so she stuck with Trinity to avoid such mistakes.

Pushing the chips aside, Trinity smiled when she found her "special" tube of lipstick. While it was completely functional, it also served as a camera when needed. With it, she could record events. Should the need arise to obtain proof of something, she had only to twist the tube the wrong way and it would activate the camera.

Surveying the area, she couldn't help but smile. Twelve of the last fourteen missions she'd been on had been strictly surveillance and that always equaled boring. The only good thing about being stuck with surveillance duty was that she wasn't expected to seduce anyone.

She was one of a dozen or so RLS-69s that had been with Simon from the beginning. The rest of the agents were fairly new and on their first or second missions. They had been trained in the art of seduction along with several styles of martial arts, weaponry, survival and just about anything else Simon could throw at them.

Though the other agents hadn't completed the entire training, they had the core portions done. Technically, since the addition of a new course, cooking, Trinity was missing that course. She'd attempted to opt out of it but Simon reminded her of the disastrous birthday dinner she'd planned for him once. The cake, or dried hunk of hard something, had been hard enough that it broke her pinky toe when she dropped it.

I'd rather seduce a man than cook him dinner and that's not saying much.

Trinity had never been comfortable in the seduction department. As much as she loved sex, she still couldn't bring herself to rub against strange men that didn't appeal to her. She did it when she absolutely had to, and she did it well. Thankfully, Simon's "seduce but don't fuck" policy gave her a good reason to end the escapades before they got out of hand. It was set into place for their protection more than anything. They were hired guns who just happened to look good in lipstick and lingerie. That didn't mean they were required to fuck their way through every mission. Some RLS-69s did use sex as a weapon, but Trinity preferred more traditional methods—knives, laser pulsars, poison, the list was really endless.

She'd only come close to breaking Simon's unofficial rule once and that was only because she'd been drugged with a poison dart on Vedieone. When she woke to find herself in a rather compromising position, she beat the living shit out of the person responsible and served his head on a platter, literally, to the King of Vedieone. With their serial killer dead, Vedieone no longer had need of the RLS-69's services and she was free to return to Restigatio. However, the king, a powerful man in his own right, had wanted her to stay. He attempted to marry her off to one of his sons. As sweet as that offer was, and as sexy as the princes were, such a destiny wasn't written in the stars for her.

No. Trinity was a lone gun now. Marriage didn't factor into the equation. The king handled the rejection of his offer to her rather well and insisted that she allow his head sorcerer to "bless her". Seeing no way out of it, Trinity had allowed it. She'd bid the king good wishes and left. Upon her return to Restigatio, she took the required downtime and then headed out on her next mission.

A buzzing began in her ear and Trinity knew that the A-mac was launching its download sequence. She swore the machine hated her. Most of the girls got their downloads on the way down. Simon said it was because her missions had more details to them.

One sharp pinch later and the information started flowing into her mind. Another sharp pinch happened. Trinity grabbed her head and moaned. It had never done that before. The information flow stopped abruptly.

This isn't a good sign.

Tapping her wrist, she again tried to contact to Simon. Nothing happened. Oh, this was very bad indeed. Trinity accessed the few files that had managed to download and was sorely disappointed in their content. Fragmented images of a man with short chestnut-colored hair and matching dark eyes appeared. As quick as his face popped up, it was gone, being replaced by a sense of danger.

Trinity was used to the warning of danger on a mission. What she was not accustomed to was the overwhelming feeling that the man was in grave danger.

Was that her mission? Was she supposed to protect this nameless stranger? The A-mac gave her a location and on a planet the size of Mixlione she could look for eons without finding him. There had to be something more. She searched her mind and found nothing. Her only hope was that the A-mac had deposited her in the vicinity of her target.

The sound of music filtered to her, and she crept toward the edge of a large building. Unsure of what she'd encounter, she edged her way toward the walkway, doing her best to keep a low profile. Equipped with only a minimal amount of weapons, she didn't feel like taking on an army, especially while dressed for a party.

"Hey, sweetness, lookin' for some action? I'd like to pound that ass a few times."

Trinity turned to find a group of men standing behind her. Where had they come from? Worse yet, what were they planning on doing? She backed up slightly, giving herself room to maneuver if need be, and smiled. It the boys wanted to play, she'd play. It would be a shame to get such a pretty dress dirty but it'd be worse to pass up the change the beat the crap out of these fools.

* * * * *

Waylon Balch pulled the busty blonde that had become his shadow at some point during the evening off him. Placing her on the stool next to him, he pushed several turquoise chips her way. Her eyes lit up.

"Are these for me?" She touched each chip tentatively as though she was afraid they'd hurt her. He'd never heard of three quadrillion mixlionions doing anything beyond setting a person up for life but he could have been mistaken.

He refrained from making any rude comments, as hard as that was, and forced a smile onto his face. "Yes, consider it an apology."

"An apology for what?" Her enhanced lips were ridiculously large and the sexy pout she was going for looked more like she'd been stung by a *gelipson* bug than alluring. The damn things infected every galaxy in the universe and no doubt would be the only thing left alive in the event that the universe would end.

"For my dismissal of you." He bit back a smile as her eyes widened. "Your services are no longer required. In fact, they were never required. I'm sorry you were led to believe I needed company. I'm sure you'll find the sum more than adequate. Feel free to discuss any further matters with my associate, Rupert."

Her mouth dropped open and she looked offended. Apparently, she wasn't used to rejection.

Too bad.

Waylon wasn't about to spend the night with her under him. For some insane reason Rupert thought he needed "company" to keep himself stress free. Not to mention their species, the *figiutatio*, were dying out and the need to procreate was high. The only problem was Rupert's choice in women. He liked his women with abnormally large breasts, fuller than average lips, dyed hair and little brains. Thankfully, none of the women to date had possessed any human DNA or Rupert could have found himself shackled to a bimbo for the rest of his immortal life.

Sure, the women Rupert selected were perfect if Waylon wanted to sink his cock into something and toss it out after use, but that wasn't what he craved. No, he wanted someone who could stand toe to toe with him in every aspect of his life—a friend, a lover, a companion, a mate. Rupert's prostitutes didn't even come close to fitting the bill.

Waylon left the woman sitting at the *pixeton* game table. If she decided to sit there and gamble away the money, it was her choice. He just wanted to get away from her as fast as he could. Her cheap perfume had been enough to make his stomach turn. He needed air and now.

"Waylon, are you there?"

He cringed at the sound of Rupert's voice through his built-in communicator. He'd forgotten to deactivate the damn thing. The last thing he wanted to do was explain his reasoning for not fucking Rupert's "company picks" again. "Yeah, I'm here."

"Well, how is she?"

Waylon pushed the casino doors open and headed out into the night. He needed to walk, to stretch his legs and clear his mind. "She's great, thanks."

"Aww, you left her at the bar, didn't you?"

Waylon smiled despite himself. "You know me well, buddy."

"I sure do and that's why I already had a backup picked out for you tonight. Before you say anything, you need to understand she's not normally what I'd pick out for you."

Waylon arched an eyebrow. If Rupert wouldn't normally select her, then there was hope she was actually a beautiful woman. Immediately, he chastised himself for even entertaining committing to an evening with a prostitute. "I appreciate the effort but I'm going to have to pass."

"I'm afraid you're too late. She should be waiting by your vehicle. She said she'd be in a little black dress and you'll love this one…she's a brunette."

"Rupert, don't you…" The transmission ended and Waylon knew Rupert wouldn't attempt to connect with him again until morning.

He increased his pace while heading to his vehicle, hoping to avoid whatever slut Rupert had selected for him. Approaching the corner of the building, Waylon heard the sound of men shouting.

"Hey, baby, you know you want to give us a free ride."

"Yeah, and I want to be the first to let her."

"No, I'm going first."

Waylon peered around the corner and spotted five men huddled near the most beautiful woman he'd ever seen. His breath caught in his chest as he fully took her in. Her long dark brown hair hung in large, loose curls down to the middle of her back. She looked up at the men with emerald green eyes. A normal humanoid would not have been able to pick out subtle details in the dark at that distance, but Waylon was anything but normal. The woman's rose-colored lips drew into a smile. She looked entirely too happy to be caught in a dark parking lot with a group of aggressive men.

Did she really want these men to take turns with her?

Glancing her over one last time, he took note of her little black dress. The girl certainly fit Rupert's description, but how the man could think she wasn't sexy was beyond him. The idea of sticking his dick in someone who'd serviced more men than she could count had always left him cold. But, staring at this prostitute, his loins burned. He waited in the shadows and watched to see if she'd fuck the group of men or not. Why it was so important to him, he wasn't sure. One thing was for certain, he couldn't tear himself away from her.

"Come on, sugar, you know you want daddy to give it to you good and hard," one man said, reaching out and grabbing her arm.

The prostitute winced. The beast within Waylon tried to surface. He had to fight it back before he went to intervene. The woman twisted fast and delivered a roundhouse kick to the man's throat. Considering she was only around five foot seven and the man she was up against was well over six feet, that was quite a feat. The man jerked backward and clutched his throat.

Another man threw a punch at her and she not only ducked out of the way, she delivered a jab to his windpipe that sent him to his knees. When the other three charged her, Waylon decided it was high time he helped out. Rushing out of the darkness, he descended upon the three men with his supernatural speed. He took two out with one sweep and the other the prostitute handled.

Waylon turned to check on her and froze as something sharp pressed against his throat. Glancing down, he found that the woman had her leg fully extended and her foot pressed against his neck. That felt awfully sharp to just be a high heel. He narrowed his gaze on her and drew in a deep breath when he realized just how drop dead gorgeous she was.

There was a classic beauty about her, with her high cheekbones and narrowed nose. He couldn't sense any enhancements on her, which meant that she came by her beauty naturally. From the pressure being applied to his throat, he got the sense that she came by a few others things as well.

She met his gaze head on and didn't flinch when he let his eyes shift from brown to pale blue and back again. That very move had sent more people running from him than he could count. This one didn't seem fazed.

"If you move, I will slit your throat."

"With your pumps?" He smiled devilishly at her and winked.

She pressed her foot harder to his throat and he felt something cutting into his skin. "No, jackass, with the blade sticking out of my pumps."

Waylon's cock hardened. Not only was she beautiful, strong and lethal, but her voice was so soft, so silky that it made him instantly think of her calling out his name as he fucked her.

Her green eyes raked over him and she eased the pressure on his neck. "Oh shit, you're him!"

Waylon seized the moment to grab her ankle and twist her around. He rode her body to the ground and pinned her. The new position did little in the way of alleviating his erection issues. If anything, having her lush ass pressed against his hard cock made it all worse. Why was he so attracted to a whore? And more importantly, where did a common streetwalker learn moves like that? "Who are you?"

"Trinity," she muttered and he realized that he was pressing too hard on her.

Easing up a bit on her, Waylon took in her light floral scent. He could have sworn that she smelled like an Earthling to him.

Knowing that was impossible, he pushed the thought from his mind. "Mmm…oh…okay, Trinity, where the hell did you learn to fight like that?"

"Restigatio."

Her answer shocked him. Restigatio was a hard-core prison planet that housed women from all over the tri-galaxy area. "Did you get busted for prostitution?"

Trinity huffed and pushed against the man on her back. If she wanted to, she could have flipped him off her without a second thought, but so far all he'd done was make her cream herself. No harm in that, right? His assumption that she'd been convicted of prostitution shocked her. "No, not exactly. Now, let me up or else."

"Or else what?" he asked, his voice sounded smug. He pressed his hard erection against her ass and her pussy clenched in anticipation. The man took a deep breath in. "Mmm, I get it. If I don't let you up, you'll keep creaming yourself until I slide in…err … I mean off you."

As much as she wanted to hit the man, she couldn't help but laugh. "Ha, ha, very funny, now let me up."

He pressed his hips against her and spread her legs more. "Say please."

Trinity gritted her teeth. "I beg no man."

"No, you just require an additional fee."

"Fuck you."

"Perhaps."

The man tensed and then rolled off her. She went to stand and found him pulling her up. Glaring at him, she adjusted her now dirty dress. "I can stand on my own, thanks. And, for the record, I didn't need your help with those men." She looked around. They were gone. "Hmm, where did they all go?"

The sexy stranger glanced around and shrugged. "Off to try to solicit sex from some other prostitute, I suppose."

Trinity's mouth dropped open. Was he implying that she was a hooker, again? Did the man ever let up? Maybe he had prostitutes on the brain or something. Whatever his deal was, he was downright annoying.

And sexy as hell.

She tried to turn and storm away from him to prove a point. What point that was remained to be seen but it didn't matter. She couldn't even tear her gaze off him much less leave his vicinity.

"What's he paying you for the night?" he asked.

Confused, she wrinkled her nose and shook her head. "Huh? Who are you talking about?"

He smiled and extended his hand. "Oh, you're good. By far the best one he's picked yet. Gods, you play the game so well that you almost make me think you're not a…oh …never mind. Anyway, I'm Waylon Balch."

Waylon. She liked the sound of that. For a minute, Trinity entertained ignoring Waylon's hand but her body betrayed her. Before she knew it, her cool hand was planted in his warm one.

He glanced down at their joined hands and smiled. "You're so tiny."

Tiny? That wasn't something she was called often. It wasn't like she was a giant or anything but she was tall—taller than many of the other agents at least. Waylon caressed her hand and she lost her train of thought.

His dark brown eyes locked on her and a devilish grin spread over his handsome face. "So, would you like to continue to stand out here in the dark or shall we head back to my place and fuck the night away?"

Trinity staggered backward and almost fell. Waylon's hold on her hand was the only thing that kept her steady and upright. Fucking the night away wasn't something she did but now it was all she could think about.

"You okay? If you would rather just fuck in my transport vehicle or even behind the casino, we can. I just assumed you'd prefer a bed. I guess women like you can do it anywhere, huh?"

"Women like…?"

Waylon leaned forward fast and captured her lips with his. All of her protests stopped as the sweet taste of his mouth consumed her. When his tongue dove in and licked along the inner edges of her lower lip, Trinity moaned and pressed her body against his.

At the moment, she'd let him think whatever the hell he wanted to think about her. She was horny and in need of a stiff cock. From the feel of what was pressing into her stomach, Waylon would more than do.

Chapter Two

Trinity stared over at Waylon, unsure why she'd gotten into his vehicle. The compulsion to see to his safety overwhelmed her. As she watched him maneuvering through the busy sections of the city, the tension she normally carried eased.

Never before had a man affected her so. On the few occasions that she'd given in to the need for sex, she'd simply selected someone she found attractive and fucked him. No questions asked. No comments. No further attraction. Could she really see herself simply fucking the man next to her then never looking back?

Not that it mattered. She was an RLS-69 operative until the end of her natural life. Other agents would only serve until their original sentence was up, but Trinity was not eligible for parole and hers was a life sentence. Though she had been sentenced to death to start with. Simon's intervention and offer of working for him stopped that. Living with Simon was not only bearable, he was the closest thing to a family she had in a very long time.

Like it or not, the RLS program owned her and falling for a man wasn't an option. It could only lead to heartache. The very thought of caring for someone and then going back to her life on Restigatio terrified her. She'd learned to numb herself to the reality of forever being alone many years ago. To let anyone under her protective shields was not only foolish, it was insane.

"Did you decide where you want to fuck?"

Trinity's mouth fell open and she bit back a rude comment. Taking two calming breaths, she forced a smile onto her face. "Do you speak this way to all the women you meet or am I just special?"

Waylon chuckled. "Special, yes, but that doesn't really change things, does it?"

"Meaning?"

"Meaning," he said, glancing over at her, "there can never be anything between us so let's just enjoy our time and make every ounce of money dropped on this meeting tonight count."

Money?

What the hell was he talking about? Why was he so convinced she was a prostitute? Was that her cover story? If so, how did he know that? It wasn't like she attempted to solicit him.

His gaze raked over her and her nipples hardened. Regardless what the man thought she was, her body wanted him, she wanted him. Did it really matter what he thought? He was right. There would never be anything between them. She was a convicted criminal and half human. A combination like that would turn any man away.

She touched his thigh and had to hold back from squeezing it. "You decide."

"It's my call, huh?" Waylon asked as his cock began to harden. Trinity's hand was so light on his leg that he wasn't even sure she was still touching him. And gods how he wanted her to touch him. He wanted to land his vehicle and fuck the hell out of her. Giving in to his animalistic nature, he made a fast left turn and pulled into a dark alley.

"Waylon?"

"Computer, lower the control panels."

Instantly, the dark gray steering column and the control dashes shifted forward, leaving a few extra feet for maneuverability. Rupert had told him countless stories of having sex with women in his transport vehicle and he was an inch or so taller than Waylon. He didn't care if his legs were so cramped that it stopped the flow of blood. He wanted Trinity. "Come here."

Seeing the hesitation in her face, Waylon thought she might actually back out. That was odd. He was rich, handsome and had a great body. As vain as it was, it was all true. Women generally threw themselves at him and here sat a women whose job was to please men, yet she seemed reserved. It was odd to say the least.

"If you'd rather…"

Trinity slid over to him fast and touched his cheek. Her hand was cool against his feverish skin. He didn't have a chance to ask her if she wanted to go back to the casino. She leaned into him and pressed her mouth to his. The taste of her sweet lips made him growl softly and pull her into his arms. She drew back from him and he mourned the feel of her soft lips.

Damn, she even tastes human.

She looked shyly up at him through hooded black lashes. His heart beat madly in his chest. Waylon fought for control, not wanting the beast he carried within to interfere with this moment of bliss. Stroking Trinity's face gently, Waylon ran the pad of his thumb over her swollen lips. "So beautiful."

She kissed his thumb gently. The green in her eyes seemed to deepen and Waylon couldn't help himself. Grabbing hold of her, he lifted her quickly and pulled her onto his lap. She yelped and he chuckled.

Why was interacting with her so easy, so natural? They were strangers yet he'd found himself happy more than once in their short time together. That wasn't normal for him.

"Mmm, this is…umm…nice," she whispered, her cool breath sliding over him.

Waylon rocked his hips against her and slid his hand down to her thigh. He caressed it, moving his hand up and under her tiny black dress. She gasped as he slid his hands even higher. When his fingers skated over the tops of her pantyhose, it was his turn to draw in a deep breath. He was so near the prize, so close to finding her heated core. His erection pressed madly against his pants, to the point it was painful. "I need to be in you."

Trinity leaned back and Waylon thought she was backing out on having sex with him. Disappointment ran through him. When she lifted her leg high in the air, he caught sight of her tiny black panties. Swinging her leg, she straddled him and moved her body forward.

She placed her arms around his neck as she rubbed herself against the bulge in his pants. "Mmm, this is even better."

He smiled. "I agree."

Trinity's mouth came down on his and he moaned. The second she rubbed her cunt against his clothed member, the beast within him tried to rise. Somehow, he managed to hold it at bay, even when Trinity reached between them and unfastened his pants.

His erection now free, it immediately sought the bounty before it. The tip of his dick pressed against her wet panties. He growled into her mouth and she pressed her body tighter to his. Sliding his hands up and under her dress, his body jerked as his fingers splayed over her luscious curves. No enhancements, nothing to clutter his heightened senses.

So soft. So smooth. So real.

Trinity reached between them and slid her panties to the side, allowing his cock access to her. He pulled her closer to him and pressed the tip of his dick to her entrance. It was as hot and wet as he thought it would be. Breaking his kiss, he looked into her green eyes. "I'm going to fuck you until you can't walk, can't move, can barely breathe. If you're not willing to take me every way for the entire night, you need to tell me now. Once I feel your pussy wrapped around me, I won't be able to stop."

She nibbled at his neck and licked a slow path to his mouth. Drawing his bottom lip between hers, her gaze met his. The sultry look in Trinity's eyes made his gut clench. The need to fuck her was overwhelming and the beast within him wanted in on the action.

Fighting a full-out shape shift into his preferred black panther form, Waylon pulled back a bit from Trinity. No woman had ever driven him to the point of changing or almost changing during sex before.

Trinity watched as Waylon seemed to distance himself from her. Her first reaction was to lean into him and slide over his cock. It was nestled beneath her dress, not open to her view, and she desperately wanted to know if it was as good as she thought it was. But Waylon's body tensed and he suddenly looked as though the thought of fucking her was painful.

Offended, she slid off him. When he made no move to hold her in place, she knew that he hadn't felt as strong a connection as she had.

Just as well.

The hair on the back of her neck began to tingle and all worries over her appeal to Waylon vanished. Her RLS training assured that she'd use all her senses to stay safe. And her limited sixth sense was telling her something was wrong.

"I'm sorry for that. I…I…just needed a minute to collect myself," Waylon said, softly.

"Think nothing of it. That seems to be happening to a lot of guys lately." She'd assumed he'd meant that he had premature ejaculation. The startled look upon his face told her she'd judged wrong.

"I do not have a problem holding off my orgasm. In fact, it's better if I do." Each word was clipped. "And just how *many* men have you been with lately?"

As much as she wanted to both hit him and soothe him, Trinity had time for neither. The sense that something was wrong increased. Glancing out of the window nervously, she did her best to see in the darkness. The only light came from the now retracted control panel and that only let off enough to allow her to see Waylon. If her suspicions that they were being watched panned out, then that meant whoever was out there could see them but they couldn't see him.

Instantly, another file from the A-mac decrypted in her head. Trinity bit back a scream as her mind accessed the broken information. A vision of a woman with long hair popped into her mind. She couldn't make out a face, but she saw the long sniper rifle in the woman's hand. An image of Waylon flooded through her, only in the vision he was spread out on the ground, not moving.

"Well, are you going to answer me?"

"No," Trinity said as she kicked into RLS mode. It was then she noticed a small fuchsia pinpoint from across the way. That was an M825y6 sniper rifle marking if she'd ever seen one. The range on the weapon was quite extensive and Trinity knew they'd never get away fast enough. "Get down!"

"Answer my damn question!"

"Sexy and stupid. Just my luck."

"Stupid?"

Shit, I said that aloud.

Knowing that his time was limited, Trinity launched herself at him, reaching for the lever that would release his seat back. She pushed off the dash with both feet, adding to the force of her body hitting his. They flipped over the seat and landed with a thud in the cargo portion of the vehicle. Waylon looked stunned beneath her and then pissed. He opened his mouth just as a blast rattled the entire vehicle.

Trinity pressed her body tight to his, hoping to shield him from any debris. Quickly, their positions changed. No longer was she the protector. Now, she was the protected. Trapped under his large body, she had little time to protest before another blast rocked them.

Waylon's brown eyes shifted to pale blue as he snarled. Trinity drew in a deep breath. It was one thing to see him do this during battle. It was another to see the trick up close and personal. Her heart raced and the instinct to fight instead of run kicked in. She brought her knee up fast, hoping to catch him off guard. When he shifted quickly, blocking her progress, she realized that catching Waylon off guard wouldn't be easy.

"Who is shooting at us and why?"

Trinity shook her head slightly. "I don't know who or why."

He bent his head down and sniffed her neck. "You lie but you don't."

Okay, that was weird.

Was she supposed to tell him the absolute truth? That she was a special agent whose planet downloads went berserk? Somehow, she didn't think he'd buy that. If he did, what would happen to her? Simon had made it very clear that disclosing the RLS-69 program was not tolerated. He and his "associates" liked their privacy. They even killed to protect it. She didn't think Simon would hurt her. Then again, she never thought he'd come in his pants while she demonstrated the art of seduction.

Waylon pressed his body against hers, causing his thick erection to dig into her. He caught hold of her wrists and pressed them above her head. "I should be angry with you. Furious, in fact. But all I can think about is fucking you senseless." He pushed harder, grinding his pelvis against the soft pad of her pussy. "That will be your punishment. I'll fuck you and then I might have to spank you for keeping things from me."

The obvious threat didn't scare Trinity one bit. It excited her, made her nipples pucker and her inner thighs tighten. She rubbed her body against his and almost begged him to take her. It didn't matter that a crazed woman with a sniper phaser was attempting to kill them. It didn't matter that Waylon didn't trust her. All that mattered was how wet her pussy was and how very much she wanted his dick in it.

"Mmm, you're wet for me. I can smell it."

Trinity was just about to comment on Waylon's bizarre choice of words when another large blast struck the vehicle. This time the impact proved to be more than the transport vehicle could withstand. Even though it was top of the line, it wasn't made for a full-on attack.

Something snapped and popped next her head. Blue and white sparks shot out of a panel near her. Trinity hissed as one of the sparks came into contact with her cheek. The sudden pain brought her back from the edge of sexual madness. Instantly she did the only thing she could think of. She slammed her head into his.

Waylon jerked back, shocked that Trinity had resorted to head-butting him. That moment afforded her the opportunity to thrust him off her. In an instant, she was at the back hatch and flipping it open. At first, he assumed she wanted away from him but when she looked back, she motioned to him.

"We need to get the hell out of here. One more shot and this could explode."

She thrust her tight little ass up in the air as she prepared to leap out of the vehicle. Waylon's cock jerked wildly, wanting him to go to her, fuck her and claim her.

Claim her?

He shook the thoughts from his head just in time for another blast to strike. Trinity reached back and seized hold of his collar. She ripped him forward and they both tumbled out onto the parking lot. Waylon rolled fast and came to his feet. He turned to help Trinity up but found her standing next to him. She flashed him a knowing smile and then looked behind them.

"She's close."

"She?"

"Follow me."

Waylon took a deep breath, soaking in the scents of the attacker. Trinity had been right. Whoever it was, was female. His supernatural senses had been dulled by lust and it was harder for him to hear now. Still, he knew the attacker was closing in on them.

While he highly doubted that a blast from a phaser, no matter what the voltage, would kill him, he knew it would kill Trinity. Why he suddenly felt the need to protect a prostitute he'd only just met was beyond him. But one thing was for certain, he'd not allow harm to come to her.

Grabbing Trinity's hand, he pulled her toward the abandoned building they'd parked behind. He was impressed that she ran as fast as she did considering how high her heels were. Most women he knew had only learned to sashay, not run a marathon in high heels.

Waylon slammed into the door and sent it crashing inwards. Trinity gasped and he knew that his strength scared her and that bothered him. He didn't want her to be afraid—he wanted her to be under him, over him, in front of him. Any way that allowed him to fuck her.

Waylon jerked her into the building with him and pulled up what limited supernatural magic he possessed to mask their presence. "She can't find us now." Trinity's breath caught and he sensed her shock. Centering his gaze on her, he smiled wickedly.

Trinity licked her lower lip and the corner of her mouth drew up. The sexy look upon her face could have sent even the strongest of men to their knees and Waylon was no exception. If he hadn't had his power raised then, he'd have fallen victim to the vixen before him. Already, he wanted to slam her against the wall and fuck her until she begged him to keep her. The idea of having her walk by his side for eternity was ludicrous.

Wasn't it?

"Surprised?" he asked, trying to keep his thoughts from such things.

She nodded, but her response wasn't what he expected. "Very, I didn't know there were others like…"

"Like who?" Waylon watched her closely, trying to sense if she would lie to him. She'd piqued his interest with that comment. Hell, she'd piqued his interest the moment he first saw her.

Trinity's gaze flickered over him as she seemed to weigh her words carefully. "Someone close to me has an energy that feels similar to yours."

An energy similar to mine?

"Explain."

She huffed and rolled her eyes. "Not that I owe you an explanation, you arrogant prick, but there's a man, an important man in my life, who can make the same buzzing, tingling feeling surround me. It also does the same thing to me."

Pangs of jealousy stabbed through him. His hands burned for the change. The beast within wanted out, wanted to be free to kill the man who dared to be close to his mate.

My mate? Oh, gods I need to get away from her. She'll be the death of me yet.

"A man?" He arched an eyebrow in question, needing to hear from her lips who this important man in her life was. "Maybe it's your father or an uncle."

Trinity snorted. "No way in hell! He's no relation to me and that's the only reason I'm close to him. He's a saint next to my uncle."

Shit.

Waylon hadn't realized he'd spoken aloud. Trinity's response only served to infuriate him more. "Are you fucking him?"

The hate that flashed through her eyes almost made him step back. He held his ground, his feet rooted firmly in place. She moved toward him, either unaware or unconcerned with the firestorm brewing within him. Her finger jabbed hard into his chest.

"Who do you think you are?" she demanded. "I don't know you and I definitely don't owe you anything, yet you expect me to answer questions about men who make me come. Do you hear me asking about your personal life? How many women have you fucked, Waylon? You seem very stuck on the whole prostitute thing. Are you into that sort of thing? Is that what it takes to get you off?"

Waylon brushed her insults aside, focusing only on her confession. "So you have fucked him."

Waving her hand in the air, she turned to go back out to the parking lot. "You're on your own, bucko."

Panic pushed past the anger. Grabbing Trinity's arm lightly, he pulled her back. Long flowing strands of dark brown hair fell over his arm and he gave in to the need to touch her again. His animalistic nature won out and he slammed her against the wall. "Yeah, baby. Fucking the hell out of you, knowing that you're required to be here will do just fine."

She opened her mouth and he took the opportunity to regain control of the situation. Pressing his mouth to hers, he licked along the edges of her lips and rubbed his body against hers. Trinity moaned into his mouth and he slid his tongue in.

Trinity tried her best to resist Waylon's kiss but ceasing to breathe would have been easier to follow through with than that. Their tongues locked and their bodies simulated sex. It wasn't long before her pussy was so wet that she felt it seeping down her inner thigh.

A sharp pain shot through her head and she found herself accessing an encrypted file without any prompting on her part. She closed her eyes. This time, she received a bit more about him. The file broke down and she hissed as the pain shot through her head again. She broke the kiss, pulling away quickly, grabbing hold of her temples. Waylon touched her shoulder and she tried to use his arm to steady herself.

Trinity blinked several times and looked up to find Waylon's deep brown eyes staring back at her. If she didn't know better, she'd have sworn he looked concerned. That was ridiculous. The man thought she sold her body for money and talked to her as one would talk to a pet they hated.

"You've got some explaining to do," he said.

Another sharp pain ripped through her head and she received another spec of data. White-hot fire lanced through her head and down her neck. Trinity grabbed her head. "Waylon...*figiutatio*...annihilation of species..."

Waylon didn't let her finish her sentence. He grabbed hold of her and shook her hard. "How the hell do you know about the *figiutatio* and who sent a prostitute to try to kill me—again?"

Trinity didn't have a chance to answer. The buzzing in her head began again, only this time it wasn't just painful, it was downright excruciating. Darkness swallowed her as a scream lodged in her throat.

Chapter Three

Trinity woke with a start and tried to sit upright in the large wood bed. Her brows drew together as she did her best to make sense of the scene. The planet was known for its trendy, state-of-the-art facilities. Not that the room wasn't beautiful. In fact, that was the problem. The room was too beautiful. It reminded her of Simon's personal quarters.

Even Restigatio had its fair share of blandness—especially within the prison itself. RLS Headquarters was different. While up-to-date and in most cases beyond innovative, Simon had found a way to give it a homey feel. Like that of the pictures Abbi had so often displayed for them of the planet Earth and how humans lived. Some of it seemed rather barbaric at times but as the planet had matured, so did its people.

Trinity wished she would've been able to see what it looked like firsthand. To know what the ocean felt like. To understand what it was like to live in one of the large homes in one of the neighborhoods that looked so much alike. Most of all, she wished she could know the love that seemed to radiate from the photos of families from that time frame.

Looking around the large room, she once again marveled at how very similar the furniture was to what Simon had in his personal quarters. He too had a wooden bed, beautiful artwork on the walls and thick fabric pinned in places that gave off an air of romance. The first time she'd ever seen anything like it had also been the first time she'd ever been in Simon's quarters.

Agents weren't permitted in Simon's personal area. He'd not only summoned her to meet him there but yelled at her to come inside. To this day, she was unsure what it was Simon had wanted. All she could remember was seeing the beauty of his home, the wonder of the paintings, the furniture, the feel. It was then that he confessed that he knew full well she was half human. And it was then Simon told her that he had ties similar to hers as well.

Pulling her thoughts away from the similarity between the room she was in now and Simon's made her take pause. Where was she? More importantly, who brought her here?

Much to her dismay, Trinity found that her wrists and ankles were bound with black cords to the tall posts of the large bed. Left spread-eagled, in only her black bra and panties, she stared around the room wide-eyed, doing her best to understand how she'd come to be here. If she had to lob another man's head off she was putting in for a month vacation. If some exotic king came forth after she did it and tried to marry her off again, she was putting in for three months.

Trinity's training taught her to remain calm at all times but in her gut she knew Waylon was in danger. Being tied up here meant that she couldn't be protecting him. She pulled hard on her wrist, trying to activate her RL-com chip. "Simon! Simon, you need to fucking pick up! Something went wrong with the mission."

"Yes, Simon, your little hooker didn't kill her target," a deep familiar voice said.

Trinity stared down the length of her body and watched in awe as Waylon appeared out of the darkness magically. He stood tall, his brown hair tousled. He'd lost the suit. In fact, he'd lost every stitch of his clothing.

Hard, rippled muscles covered his upper body, giving way to even more ridges on the path downward. Her gaze went to his ruddy cock and her mouth gaped as she saw the sheer size of it. The scary thing was, Waylon wasn't even hard yet and he was bigger than she'd ever seen before. Fully erect, he would be downright terrifying.

"Like what you see there? Or see so many in your line of work that they all sort of run together?"

"What? Huh?" She tore her gaze away from his cock, directing it back up his washboard abs and tawny chest.

Oh, that's not helping matters. Maybe I could beg to be blindfolded.

Waylon crawled onto the bed and she jerked, trying to free herself but not really wanting to get away. Her body sizzled with desire and she hoped that his plans were to ravish her. Gods willing, she'd ravish him if she was able to get free.

A feral smile crept over his handsome face. "Who is Simon?"

Shit!

Others weren't supposed to know about Simon and the RLS-69 program. It wouldn't do a lot of good if the entire galaxy knew to watch out for undercover females. Deciding that avoidance was the best policy, Trinity tried to change the subject. "What's a *figiutatio*?"

Waylon stopped and stared down at her. He tipped his head slightly, appearing to size her up. When his lips drew tight, she expected the worst. "You should know. After all, you were sent to seduce and then kill me."

"What?" That didn't sound like a mission Simon would send her on. Okay, so it did sound a little like her missions, but still, he wouldn't have loaded files that portrayed Waylon in a victim manner. Something was wrong.

He touched her inner thigh and grinned. A claw erected from the tip of his finger and scraped hard against her skin. Amazingly, she didn't scream. She jerked, thinking he was going for her femoral artery. But for some reason he didn't even break the skin. Not that she wanted him to.

Waylon looked up at her with pale blue eyes and snarled. Trinity tried in vain to free herself from the cords that bound her. Each pull, each tug only left her wrists sore and her fingers numb.

A deep laugh came from Waylon, sounding anything but human. He licked his lips and his tongue seemed longer than it should. His teeth were definitely sharper than they should've been. He moved his body completely over hers, pressing his thick erection against her stomach as he licked her cheek. She stared up at him with wide eyes and waited for him to rip her throat out.

"What's the matter, Trinity? Cat caught your tongue?" He snarled again, this time he sounded exactly like a large wild cat—like the ones she'd seen on so many clips from her RLS courses on animals of the worlds, past and present. He nuzzled his face into her neck and took in a deep breath. She waited for pain to follow. None did. Only pleasure tore through her as he pressed his hips harder against her, rubbing her clit through her thin panties.

He felt so good, so right, but he was a deadly predator—a species she wasn't familiar with and that scared her. Being scared wasn't something Trinity did often. So far, she not only feared him, she'd feared for him as well. What did that mean? Did she see him as more than a mission?

Falling for a man was something she'd never done. As Waylon continued to grind himself against her, she did her best to keep her emotional shields up. They held, barely.

Waylon brought his face up and although his eyes were still a pale blue, his mouth seemed to be back to normal. It was a good thing too, because he dropped his head down and seized hold of her lips. He forced his tongue into her mouth and she welcomed it.

Gods, he tasted good.

He ran his fingers down her inner arms and propped himself up in a semipush-up. "Tell me who hired you."

Trinity stared at him, unable to respond through her lust-filled haze. Waylon apparently took that as a sign of resistance because he ripped open her bra and took her nipple into his mouth. He bit down, just this side of too hard. Cream lined her panties. He looked up at her as he began to suck gently on it, soothing the ache he'd placed there, and she couldn't stop herself from moaning. The minute he pulled his head from her, he took his warmth and left her nipple erect and aching.

"Who hired you?" He moved down her body, covering it with tiny kisses and warm caresses. He nibbled on her flesh, tasting it with a tenderness that surprised her. When he reached the top of her panties he smiled. "I love looking at your come-soaked pussy. I've never seen a woman cream this much before. You can try to fight me but the evidence of how much you want me to cram my dick in you is right here."

Embarrassed enough as it was, Trinity looked toward the wall. Waylon tore her panties free from her body and she flinched. It wasn't out of fear. No, regardless how helpless she was at the moment, she wanted him. She wanted to see to it that he was happy as well and being tied to the bed seriously limited her abilities to please him.

Waylon licked Trinity's cunt and sent fire jolting throughout his body. She tasted so good. So sweet. So ready to receive him. Flickering his tongue over her clit caused her to cry out. He chuckled into her pussy and continued on with his sexual exploration. She would cave soon. He just hoped it wasn't too soon. He wanted to fuck her and hiding under the guise of extracting information from her made it easier on his conscience.

Her pink pussy was even sexier than he'd pictured. And oh, how he had pictured it. He'd brought her home with him instead of to the authorities in hopes to sneak a peek at it. In truth, he'd only tied her up to prevent her from attacking him. It wasn't until he'd heard her calling for "Simon" that the primal urge to take her, claim her, fuck her came over him.

Not one prone to jealousy, Waylon was shocked by his response to Trinity. She was a prostitute and to top it off, she'd been sent to kill him. It'd been a long time since his enemies had attacked and even longer since they tried to use a female to do their bidding. The last one didn't work because he could smell the evil in her.

It was both a gift and a curse, being a *figiutatio* warrior. He was one of the lucky ones though. His powers only extended to shifting into various cat breeds, speed, strength and partial empathy. Other *figiutatio* had many more powers to contend with. Still others, like Rupert who'd not been a warrior, had an altogether different sort power. Waylon wasn't even sure he knew what his friend was capable of.

As he licked along Trinity's drenched folds, he drew in her sweet scent. Damn, she tasted every bit as good as she looked. Why the fuck did he have to fall for a woman sent to destroy him—to try to put an end to his line of people?

Her swollen bud called to him and he sucked on it gently. Inserting a finger into her cunt, he was shocked to find how tight she was. For a whore, he expected her to be too loose to do anything with. No. Trinity was tight, damn near virgin-like. Fucking her would be a prize for him. Seeing her pussy lips spread to accommodate him would make it all worth it.

She bucked beneath his touch as he worked a second finger into her. She cried out and he licked her clit more, hoping to stimulate her body into producing more cream. Why he was concerned about pleasing her was beyond him. But he was. For whatever reason, he didn't want harm to come to her. He wanted to see the look on her face as he made her climax. The thought of her being the one to end his long existence tore at his gut.

I want to keep you. Why?

She didn't answer his unspoken question and that was fine by him. Waylon pushed the feelings down and concentrated on the bounty before him. He finger-fucked her tight little pussy and licked her sweet bud until she came hard and fast on his face. A stream of fluid burst free from her, coating his chin as she tried to clamp her legs shut. It was so rare to find a woman who could ejaculate too. It was most certainly unforgettable—as everything with Trinity was.

Licking her cream from his face, he stared up at her, expecting to see at least some fear on it—he did have her tied up and was having his way with her after all. There was no fear, only lust, passion and sleepy bedroom eyes.

Waylon's cock throbbed, needing release and soon. Rising to his knees, he stared down at her open cunt and entertained the thought of driving himself deep into her. That wouldn't be good. Doing that would only make the bond he felt to Trinity stronger.

Bonding with the woman sent to assassinate him wasn't a wise move. Once bonded, he could never take it back. Being mated to the bringer of his death could only lead to heartache. Still, her pussy called to him, beckoning him to take refuge in her quim and to fill her with his seed. The need to sire a son, to fill her with his child was so strong that it was almost painful. The need to make her his own, to possess her from here until infinity was even worse. If she didn't succeed in killing him, his need for her would.

"Ahh," Trinity panted, pushing her hips up and toward him.

She smelled of desire and passion. That didn't surprise him. What did was the smell of purity tainted by something dark. He grabbed hold of his cock, stroked it and glanced up at her. Her green eyes locked on his groin region and his body shook. Watching her watch him jack off was almost too much. Pinching the base of his cock tight, he managed to head off his orgasm.

"Do you like that, Trinity? Do you like watching me touch myself?"

She bit her lower lip and nodded. It was odd how shy the "ass-kicking street walker" seemed to be now. If his keen supernatural senses hadn't picked up on her attraction to him, he would have never let things go so far. He'd have turned her over to the authorities and claimed she was a mad woman spouting nonsense about *figiutatio*, a fictitious race of supernaturals that descended from Earth. No one on Mixlione would ever believe her. They understood gambling and they understood gambling-related murders and that was it.

"Answer me. Do you like watching me touch my cock?"

"Yes...yes."

"I want to have your lips wrapped around it as I mouth-fuck you. Does that scare you?"

She shook her head. "No."

"Would you take it all the way down your throat and swallow my come?"

A scared look passed over her face as her glance slid down his body. Pumping the massive member in his hand, he smiled when he realized that his size must scare her. He pinched the tip of his cock and pre-come trickled from it. "Soon, you'll lick this off me before I fuck that luscious mouth of yours. Then you'll swallow every last drop of me. You'll take me, every inch of me."

It took all his might not to slide into her and fuck her like an animal. The cords that held her bound to the bed also kept her from being able to move. While that sounded good in the beginning, it was pure torture to him now. Gripping his shaft, he rubbed it along her soaked cunt. She squirmed and grunted.

"What do you want?" He let a sly smile play across his face.

Trinity stared down at him. Her emerald green eyes seemed to stare through to his very soul.

"You," she whispered.

As much as he longed to hear that, he knew he couldn't trust her. He laughed. "You expect me to believe you want to be fucked by the man you were sent to kill?"

Trinity shook her head and began to speak. Waylon jabbed his fingers into her pussy, cutting her off before she could spew her lies. He fucked her hard and fast with two fingers and smiled as she cried out. Each tug of the cords that bound her served to remind him of his need to keep an emotional distance from her. Unable to stop himself, Waylon stroked his cock with his free hand as he thrust his fingers in and out of her.

Just slide it in. Fuck her. Take her. Claim her.

Fighting off his animalistic desires was extremely hard. He was a warrior. He could stand up to one beautiful female. Right?

"Please...please fuck me, Waylon. Oh, yes...please...fuck me."

Waylon's balls tightened and he jerked forward. Come shot out of his dick and all over Trinity's stomach. He grasped his cock tight and pumped it feverishly, making more semen fly out at her. The sight of her soaked in his juice was too much. Her skin glistened with a sheen he had created, a sheen that he'd wanted desperately to be in her cervix, filtering through it on its way to planting the seed of their future.

The beast within him rose to the surface fast. In a flash, he was off the bed and into the shadows where he shifted into full cat form. He'd been so intent on intimidating Trinity when he'd first entered the room and now he hid out of her sight as he stood in black panther form.

Trinity jerked harder at her restraints and for a moment Waylon thought she might actually break them. She didn't. He felt bad for leaving her drenched in his come, but going to her now would only make her terrified of him. And that was something he didn't want his mate to be.

My mate?

Chapter Four

Waylon stroked his cock at the sight of Trinity spread out on the bed before him. She looked so beautiful with her dark brown hair fanned out around her in long loose curls. He kissed her cheek gently, needing to be close to her again.

Throughout the course of the night, he'd kept her held with his limited magical powers in a state of sleep. Though it had been for his own protection, he had to admit that he liked being able to fully touch her and play with her. He'd first attempted to simply wipe his semen from her smooth stomach but found he couldn't stop there. No. He felt compelled to clean every inch of her. He'd even gone so far as to rub her body with scented oils.

The need to tend to her was an odd feeling for Waylon. He wasn't nurturing by nature. No warrior was. That was one of the reasons that many *figiutatio* warriors came equipped with some empath form of power. It aided in their ability to stay human.

Whatever that meant.

The *figiutatio* were anything but normal humans. Limited numbers of normal Earthlings had escaped the planet before the final explosion of the Cleansing Wars. Whoever had been left on the planet during the nuclear bombing had died instantly.

Once, his people had been many. Now, they were so few in number that he knew of only a handful that still existed. The others had either perished or had hidden themselves away so tightly that they would never be discovered again. It was possible more existed but to date, but Waylon hadn't met any.

It saddened Waylon to think that Trinity had been sent to kill him. His death was one thing, taking another able male from the *figiutatio* line was another matter. Removing him meant that there was one less chance a child would be born to one of his kind. A child and wife were something sacred to his people, something that meant the survival of their race—their legacy.

Trinity moaned softly as he pulled the sheer fabric over her head. He'd sent for a nightgown for her. When he realized that he would be forced to untie her if he didn't use his magic, he opted for leaving her bound. Waving his hands in the air, he caused the material of the nightgown to separate. It reformed around Trinity's shapely body and Waylon's gut clenched.

"You are so beautiful. So pure yet so tainted by darkness. How is it that I did not meet you sooner? I could have saved you from a life of selling your body for money and taking the lives of others."

She didn't respond to his voice. Not that he even expected her to. His magic, while low in the scope of his kind, was more than powerful on a human. Leaning down, he kissed her sweet lips. Moving to her closed eyelids, he planted tiny kisses on them as well. With considerable restraint, Waylon pulled away from her.

"If circumstances were different, beautiful one, you would be my choice for the mother of my children—my wife. And when I love, it's with all my heart, all my soul."

* * * * *

Trinity woke slowly. Pain shot through her arms and legs. Remembering she was bound to the bed, she sighed. How could she have forgotten something so important as being tied up? Sadly enough, she already knew the answer to that.

After Waylon had disappeared, she'd laid there on the verge of tears, wanting him to return, to make love to her, to finish what he'd started. When she realized he wasn't coming back, her eyes drifted shut and she let her body rest. Conserving energy was important, especially if she was still going to try to escape.

Taking a deep breath in, she noticed the soft scent of roses. She looked down, expecting to see Waylon's dried semen on her. Instead, she saw that she was not only clean but wearing a sheer white gown. The soft floral scent was coming from her. Someone had rubbed her down with it.

"What? Who…?" She glanced around the room, frantic for just one more glimpse of Waylon before she attempted her escape. Finding no sign of him, she pulled hard on her wrist, hoping to turn on her RL-com chip. Hoping he could, by some miracle, hear her, she stated loudly, "Damn it, Simon, get your ass down here. My charge thinks you sent me to kill him. You better not have or you can take this fucking job and shove it up your ass. It will be a cold day in hell before I hurt him. Sure, he's a cocky jerk who keeps thinking I'm here to whack him, and yes, that's from Abbi's classes too but that doesn't mean he needs to be hurt. He's a good man, Simon."

Glancing at the cords that held her pinned to the bed, Trinity rolled her eyes.

"Umm, okay, aside from the tying me up thing and accusing me of selling my body for a living, he's a good man. I won't hurt him. I don't care if they give me to an *Exhilgier* beast for execution. That ought to tell you something. If I'm willing to go up against a three-headed, horned, buffalo-sized beast that secretes toxins that rot flesh instantly to make its victims easier to digest, then you should know I'm pissed. I won't do it. You better hope for your sake that my mission is to protect him or you won't have to worry about needing red handbags to cover yourself because you won't have anything to cover! I refuse to hurt him and I want to come back. It'll be bad enough to leave him now as it is. Staying longer will make it impossible. Damn you, is this stupid com link working? Simon, would you answer…"

A dark shadow moved over her and she stopped trying to communicate with Simon and started trying to free herself. Jerking hard on her arm, she felt her shoulder pop. Trinity screamed out as pain tore through her. The dark shadow grew thicker and hovered just above her body. She pulled on the cords again, this time the pain was so excruciating in her shoulder that she almost threw up. Closing her eyes, she bit back another scream as a tear rolled down her cheek.

"Be still."

The sound of Waylon's voice surprised her. Peeking out, she found him naked and next to her on the bed. Gritting her teeth through the pain, she wondered how much of her conversation with Simon he'd heard.

He reached out to touch her shoulder and she cringed.

The sad look that passed over his face made her stop. It was quickly replaced by one that scared the hell out her. "What do you think you're doing? You've dislocated your shoulder. And for what purpose? You're still tied to the bed, now you're just tied and in pain. Are you happy with yourself?" He made a move to touch her again and she glared at him. Was he back to work her up and leave her craving his touch, needing to find release and longing to be near him again?

"I'm fine. Don't touch me and don't try to use the freaky eye thing on me again!"

He grunted. "You are hardly fine, woman."

"Don't put your hands on me again, you monster!"

Waylon jerked back and looked as though she'd struck him. As victorious as it was, it did little to make her feel better.

"If you do not want my help, then *fine*," he bit the last word out.

Trinity locked gazes with him and thought about defying him once more. The pain that continued to stab at her made her rethink that stance. Sighing, she tried to relax. "I want your help."

Waylon cocked his head to the side and smiled. "What?"

She rolled her eyes. "I want your help."

I want you.

"But I'm a monster," he whispered, watching her carefully. Guilt washed over her. "Think hard, Trinity. Do you really want a monster touching you?"

Gods, yes. Touch me everywhere.

She bit her lower lip and for a moment kept her eyes averted from his piercing gaze. "You're not a monster."

His brow furrowed as he seemed to be judging her, examining her for the truth. "What?"

"You're not a monster, Waylon, and I want you…err…umm, I want your help."

The corners of his mouth twitched as a tiny glint in his eyes appeared. He was laughing on the inside, she knew it. It didn't matter though. She meant what originally came out of her mouth. She wanted him.

"That's what I thought you said." He touched her shoulder lightly. Waylon's fingertips barely grazed her, yet she saw his hand there, knew she should feel pressure, even pain, something to indicate he was indeed touching her. There was nothing. Was he dulling it? Did he have the power to ease her pain?

One loud pop later and he removed his hands. She stared at her shoulder, expecting to still find it dislocated. It was completely healed. "How? Waylon, that's amazing."

Waylon shrugged as though this was a common everyday occurrence. "I've always been able to do it." He reached up and touched the cord around her wrist. When he ran his fingers over skin, she winced slightly. The skin there was raw but she didn't want him to see her pain anymore than he already had. "I caused this."

She bit back a "well obviously" and averted her gaze. Of course he'd caused it. She hadn't tied herself to the bed. Though she'd be more than willing to if it meant he would finally be inside her, fucking her the way she longed to be fucked.

Sighing, Waylon took hold of her wrist. He kissed it gently and heat poured through it. The cord gave way. Normally, she would have seized that moment to strike out and kill whoever was nearest. But hurting Waylon would be like opening her own vein—not an option one took willingly. He leaned over the top of her and his bare chest rubbed over her breasts. Instantly, her nipples hardened to tiny peaks, each desperate for his mouth, his finger, anything he was willing to offer them.

Waylon froze and she thought he might reconsider untying her. The very sight of his massive upper body spread across her was too much. Part of her wanted to stay there, be his captive as long as it meant she would finally be with him. The rest of her knew she'd never survive being separated from him if she allowed herself to become any more attached to him. Waylon had some sort of power over her.

Trinity ran her free hand down his side and drew in his manly scent. Moisture pooled between her legs and she bit back a moan. He released her other wrist and held it tight as heat flared through it.

"There," he said, pulling back from her. He leaned down, toward her feet, and twisted just enough that his cock showed.

Seeing his sex before her face, so close that she could almost touch it, was too much. She wanted to taste him. Memorize his scent and know that she caused him pleasure. When he'd ejaculated on her stomach she'd wanted desperately to be able to run her fingers through it, taste it, savor it. But her restraints had kept her from living out that fantasy.

Trinity couldn't help herself. She took hold of his cock and tried to bring it to her mouth, but her feet still being bound prevented her from reaching him. Waylon froze under the weight of her touch. She waited for him to yell, to revert back into his hostile exterior, but he didn't. Instead, he grabbed her ankles and repeated his healing procedure on both.

Slowly, he slid the gown up her legs and she smiled as she turned into him. The length of his flaccid cock was impressive and Trinity wanted to take the chance to have all of him in her mouth while she still could. When fully erect, Waylon would be too big for her. Licking around the edges of his dark brown curls, Trinity jerked when he moved the gown over her hips and spread her legs wide. Thinking he was about to roll her over onto him, she yelped when he rolled onto her.

His cock hung right above her face. Waylon's sac dipped toward her and his masculine scent made her eyelids flutter. Before she knew it, her tongue was on him, caressing his sac tenderly. His soft moan told her that he liked it. Trinity wanted him to more than like it. She wanted him to love it.

Sucking in slowly, she drew one of his balls into her mouth and wrapped her arms around his thighs. He tasted so good. Too good. No man had done this to her before. Their scents had turned her stomach, made her want to end it all then and there, but Waylon was different. The taste of his manly smelling sac made her ache for more. Could she really take more? What would happen when he was fully erect and in her mouth? Would he suffocate her? A bit panicked, she tried to slide out from under him.

Waylon laughed softly and kissed around her nether lips. "I won't hurt you, Trinity. I promise."

How had he known she was nervous? His cock began to grow. Not wanting to miss her chance at taking all of him, she twisted her head enough to take his shaft into her mouth. Waylon's body tensed above her as she continued on. His girth made her have to work a bit harder to get her mouth to accommodate him. When she finally managed to get all of him in her mouth, she arched her neck and sucked on him. He tasted so good.

Reaching up, she massaged his balls gently, rolling each one around smoothly before pressing against the skin between his anus and sac. Instantly, his cock hardened, lengthening to the point it hit the back of her throat, making her gag reflex kick in.

Oh gods, I'll choke to death.

A manly chuckle came from Waylon as he lifted his hips slightly, calming her fears. She took hold of the base of his cock, using it as added sensation for him as well as a nice stopping point to prevent him from ramming it all the way down her throat. Trinity was happy with her decision when Waylon began to suck on her clit and finger-fuck her. When she began to move her hips, he mirrored her, fucking her mouth slowly at first, then more aggressively as her pending orgasm built.

His warm tongue delved into her core and he pressed his face against her sex. The feel of Waylon's mouth on her pussy was so intense that she cried out with his dick still in her mouth more than once. The feel of his hands separating her ass cheeks slowed her pace a bit but the pure pleasure of having him deep in her mouth, fucking her freely, outweighed any questions she had formed.

Waylon's fingers moved dangerously close to her anus. Slowly, she felt him rim her and he flicked his tongue over her clit. Many screams of need and want dissolved over his cock as she thrashed beneath him. Every muscle tightened and she surrendered to Waylon in that moment, knowing that leaving him would be the hardest thing she would ever have to do.

Moaning beneath him, Trinity bucked as her legs tightened and toes curled. The movement caused her to take more of Waylon's cock than she thought she could handle and he hit the back of her throat once more. Surprisingly, she didn't gag this time. No. This time she hummed in pleasure against his rock-hard shaft while her climax struck.

Waylon pumped harder, fucking her mouth as other men had her pussy. He stiffened and began to pull back off her. Trinity grabbed his ass and held his hips to her as best she could. Her attempt was good enough—Waylon's balls pulled up and his cock pulsated as he shot come down her throat. Each salty wave of it slid into her mouth and made her hungry for more.

Waylon rubbed her clit and brought on another orgasm. He continued to stimulate her swollen bud and the pleasure was almost unbearable. She wanted to plead with him to stop but she didn't want to miss a minute of sucking him.

Trinity, are you there? Trinity?

The sound of Simon's panic-stricken voice in her head made her pause.

Answering him was impossible with Waylon's dick still in her mouth so she merely grunted.

Trinity, is that you?

She grunted again.

Trinity…can…you…Tri…

The receiver embedded behind her ear ceased to pick up any additional signals from Simon. Waylon pulled off the top of her slowly, taking his glistening dick with him. Trinity licked it once more for good measure just before it was out of reach.

Waylon slid onto his back and stared up at the ceiling.

What the hell did I just do?

He knew the answer to that. He'd just started the mating process with Trinity. A woman who, up until he'd overheard her trying to communicate with "Simon" again, he'd suspected of being a prostitute and an assassin. She never actually denied she was either. He'd not heard the entire communication, only part of it. Was she a hooker? Did Simon hire her to come to him? If so, why? It wasn't like she couldn't still be that but she didn't *feel* like a threat—at least not to him.

Having learned to rely on his senses centuries ago, Waylon listened to them. They were picking up that while Trinity did harbor a darkness in her, she wasn't there to hurt him. If anything, she seemed to radiate a different type of feeling for him altogether. One he wasn't willing to explore further just yet.

Upset with himself for giving in to his primal urge to mate with Trinity, Waylon covered his face with his arm and groaned. He felt Trinity moving on the bed.

"Aren't you afraid that I'll try to kill you?" she asked, her voice every bit as sexy as he remembered it.

The tiny bit of anger he sensed in it tore at his insides. He owed her an explanation. He owed her something. "No."

"That's all you have to offer?"

"Yes."

That's all I can offer, baby.

She huffed and moved off the bed. "Well, it *is* every day that men tie me up, have their way with me, all the while accusing me of trying to assassinate them. I guess I should be used to it by now."

The pain in her voice was evident but Waylon didn't comment on it. He couldn't. He'd let things go too far between them as it was. He should have fucked the blonde girl Rupert first sent. At least then he wouldn't have accidentally begun the mating process with her.

Accidentally? Who am I kidding? I wanted to leave my dick in her and claim her with my come. I also wanted to sink my teeth into her flesh and mark her as mine.

Disgusted that he'd let the beast within him control his actions after spending so long remaining in control of it, he rolled off the bed and stalked toward the door. Waylon stopped long enough to glance back at Trinity. She looked so beautiful in the nightgown he'd dressed her in after bathing her. Her long hair was a bit tousled and that only added to her appeal. Her cheeks were flushed and her green eyes were hard. Hurt. Anger. Pain. All her emotions washed over him, forcing him to look away to avoid rushing to her.

"Do you want to leave now? I understand if you do."

When she didn't respond, he chanced another look at her. Her eyes were slightly red and glistening. Unshed tears filled them and if she dared let one fall, he knew he'd never hold himself back from going to her. And distance was what was needed. His powers of empathy told him this feeling of vulnerability was foreign to her, or at least not something she felt on a regular basis. How had he managed to strip a woman who had acted so fiercely in battle down to the shell before him?

Because she cares for you.

He fought back against the feelings he'd picked up from Trinity. Exploring his feelings for her would never lead to anything productive so he buried them deep. The warrior in him, while rusty from nonuse, was still there, still preventing him from being able to properly express his emotions or to trust what had been laid before him.

"Do you want to stay or go? The question is a simple one."

One lone tear fell down her soft cheek. She wasn't a crier. No. Her rough exterior wouldn't allow for it, just as his didn't. Instantly, Waylon found himself moving with inhuman speed across the bedroom. He wondered if she would try to attack him or perceive him as a threat to her. She didn't. Trinity merely stood her ground as her lip trembled.

Lifting her in his arms, Waylon pulled her close to his body. Trinity tried to push against him and he sensed her embarrassment.

"I want to go," she said softly. "I never wanted to be here to begin with."

Waylon would have been stunned by her words, but he could sense the lies in them. She wanted to stay with him as much as he wanted her to. Walking their bodies back toward the bed, he laid her down on it gently. The sheer fabric of her gown did little to hide her pebble-hard nipples. He pressed his body to hers and knew that he'd take her now — he'd sample her flesh and never be satisfied with another again. It no longer mattered. All that mattered was sinking his cock deep within her womb and filling it with seed.

He growled as he tasted her sweet lips. "Mmm, you are so wrong for me, yet I want you so much."

Trinity answered him with a kiss of her own. It was so full of emotion that Waylon's dick stood at full attention and he was positive he could fuck her straight through the sheer gown if need be. Taking it off seemed like a waste of time. But he eased it up her body anyway. She spread her legs wide and pulled at the back of his head.

"Take me, Waylon."

"I'll not only take you, I'll fuck you unconscious, baby."

The glint in her eyes told him how much Trinity would enjoy it and he couldn't wait any longer. Running his hand down her body, he found her core. She was still wet from him eating her out. Trinity, as tight as she was, wouldn't be able to accommodate his size in one hard thrust. He knew it would take some working but he was a patient man—at least he'd been prior to meeting her. His fingers trembled as he took hold of his shaft. Positioning the mushroom-shaped head of it with her vagina, he stared into her eyes.

"Fuck me, Waylon. Oh gods, please."

He had every intent of taking it slow with her, easing her open, but hearing her beg him to fuck her sent him spiraling into a sea of lust, need, passion. Waylon plowed his cock into her and she screamed out below him. For a moment he couldn't move, couldn't breathe. The walls of her pussy fisted his shaft, seeming to pull it in more. Already he could tell he'd run out of room but he was happy. His balls were buried to the hilt and he couldn't ask for more. Didn't have to.

No. Trinity's tight, wet cunt could leave a man in a state of nirvana and it probably had. Quickly, he thrust the doubts he had about her out of his head and concentrated on controlling his rhythm.

"Ahh," Trinity purred as she wrapped her legs around his waist. The feel of Waylon's impressive dick in her was too much. Pain radiated from her cunt and she wiggled under him to free herself. All she succeeded in doing was rubbing her clit against his toned body. The added stimulation mixed with his long sweeping strokes quickly replaced the pain with pleasure.

Tingles moved down her legs. She was on the edge of culmination and there was nothing she could do to prevent it. Drowning in Waylon's thrusts and kisses, Trinity felt her shields crumble around her. She was in love and there was no way out.

"You feel so good, Trinity. So tight." Waylon kissed her neck softly, continuing to pump his cock in and out of her. "I'm so close, baby. So close to filling you full of my seed. I'm going to ram my dick in you so hard and far that you'll accept every fucking ounce of it."

Hearing his promise of filling her, Trinity gave in to the pending orgasm. It ripped through her, eliciting tiny animal sounds from her along the way. Waylon shifted his hips a bit, hitting her sweet spot and sending body-racking tremors through her. She grabbed the sheets, clawing at them in an attempt to ground herself.

Waylon stiffened above her. His face went slack. Complete abandonment crossed his features as he impaled her one last time with his cock. He held it to her tight and she felt his come shooting out of him in searing hot spurts. Quickly, his eyes shifted to blue and he closed them tightly.

"Ahh...take every last drop, baby, every last drop," he whispered as he laid his body fully on hers.

Trinity stroked his back and kissed his shoulder. He shuddered and more come shot into her. Expecting Waylon's cock to go flaccid, she was surprised when it hardened within her, filling her with more of his seed. "Waylon?"

He chuckled into the bed before kissing her ear softly. "You're not the only one with secrets, sweetheart."

She squirmed beneath him, well aware that her body couldn't handle anymore from him. If luck was on her side, she'd be able to walk tomorrow. As luck had never really paid her any heed, she was sure she'd have to crawl.

Waylon withdrew from her, making a wet sucking sound as he went. Seizing hold of her waist, he flipped her over onto her stomach fast. She grimaced as his fingers moved into the crevice of her ass.

"Has a client ever taken you here?" he asked, rimming her anus.

"No...I'm not..." The sentence caught in her throat as Waylon inserted his finger into her tight portal. It popped, sending blinding pain throughout her. Still he pressed on.

Another pop happened and Trinity did the only thing she could think to do, she screamed out.

Instantly, she felt the warm wet presence of something on her ass. Glancing back, she saw that Waylon's face was pressed against her buttocks. He licked the line between her cheeks and nibbled playfully at her flesh, allowing her to relax a bit more while he worked his finger in and out of her. "I want to fuck your ass, honey. Every time I look at you, I want to mount you, take your ass and fuck it until you beg me to stop."

Trinity's eyes widened. His finger had hurt bad enough, having a dick the size of Waylon's crammed up her ass would split her in two, rip her wide open. "No…no more."

Twisting slightly, she tried to get to her hands and knees. Her clit rubbed against the bed and her body betrayed her. Her nipples went hard as her pussy moistened.

Waylon chuckled and lifted her up a bit. "I can smell how aroused you are, Trinity. You want me to stick my cock in you again, don't you?"

Shaking her head no should have been easy. It wasn't. All she could do was whimper as he inserted another finger into her ass and pressed his dick against her vagina.

"That's right, baby. First I'm going to get my dick good and wet. And then I'm going to ram it in this gorgeous ass."

The air around her shifted and she felt power rolling off him. Like Simon, he made the hairs on her arm stand on end and her libido go into overdrive. Suddenly, the idea of having Waylon's huge cock spearing her ass didn't sound so bad.

Pushing back, she forced her pussy over his shaft and he gasped. The fingers fucking her ass increased in their speed while he began to work his dick in and out of her. The pleasure was more than Trinity could bear and she bucked against him madly, thrusting herself onto him, leaving him no choice but to fuck her hard and fast.

Strange cries broke free from her throat and Waylon followed with grunts of his own. He pulled out of her fast, leaving her womb feeling empty.

"No," she whimpered.

"I'm not going anywhere but in your ass, honey. Don't worry, I'll make you come again."

Before she could protest, Waylon pushed his cock into her ass, spreading her to the brink as he went. Thankfully, he eased himself in, seeming to understand the need for her to adjust to his size.

"Relax, baby, push down and relax."

Trinity did as she was instructed and exhaled as her rectum relaxed, allowing Waylon to speed his descent. Reaching around, he tweaked her clit as he fully sheathed his dick within her. Drawing in air was difficult with her engorged clit being stroked and her ass being filled but somehow she managed.

The second that Waylon increased his speed, pulling back and them pummeling into her, she gave in to the need to pant. He pinched her bud softly before rubbing it hard and fast. Her pussy clenched down, causing her ass to do the same thing. Waylon cried out from behind her and stayed rooted in place as her orgasm struck. His followed suit and she felt the hot waves of his semen filling her.

Waylon held her hips tight to him and whispered words she couldn't make out in a language she didn't recognize. Instantly, her mind fogged and her body arched back to form to his. He kissed her neck, softly sliding his tongue out and over her skin. Beyond that, neither of them tried to move.

Chapter Five

Waylon lay in bed, holding Trinity. Her hair was still damp from their shower and the vision of her sucking on his cock while the water jetted over her smooth skin had been digging at him from the moment they'd returned to bed.

She was so beautiful. Her body reacted to his as no other woman ever had. Sure, he'd made them all come but never before did his *figiutatio* powers make a woman so sexually charged that she could barely contain herself. This was a double-edged sword. As hot and horny as Trinity got, it paled in comparison to what he felt around her.

The need to take her, mark her, claim her had been so intense that he'd almost left the room, but the thought of missing one second of being with her ripped at his heart. When he'd recited the binding words as his cock was still buried deep within her ass, he'd almost done it. He'd almost sunk his teeth into her shoulder for all the universe to know she was his. No man would be permitted to touch her, let alone pay for her services. He could offer her another life, a life off the streets. Whatever reasons she had for selling her body for money were unknown to him and if he had his way, he'd find out.

This is insane. There's no future with us. We can never have children, never really be a truly mated pair.

As his thoughts plagued him, he remembered the magic that had risen around them after he'd chanted the binding words in her ear. Thankful that Trinity didn't know Latin, he waited to see what would happen. When the air around them thickened, Trinity went limp in his arms.

Somehow, he'd managed to mix essences with her, forever linking them, but he hadn't finished all that needed to be done.

He'd given her his seed, expelling more energy than he should have. But still, he managed to hang onto his gifts, at least for a little bit. After he'd done the binding, his body was as weak as hers. Though he didn't pass out, he did ease them to the bed and wrap his body around hers until the ill effects of spilling his seed passed.

Several gut-wrenching hours passed as he body was forced to adjust to his missing supernatural gifts. His muscles ached. His senses dulled and it felt as if he was moving through quicksand. Slowly, he regained his energy and his powers. It was then that he lifted Trinity's still sleeping form and carried her to the bathroom. She woke to find him holding her close to him as he adjusted the water temperature.

Waylon hadn't planned on fucking her again but once her gaze met his, he found himself spellbound. He not only fucked her, he fucked her every way imaginable. They'd stayed locked together until the water was ice cold and he could barely stand.

Somehow, the normal depletion of his powers wasn't as severe the second time around. He'd heard of other *figiutatio* being able to reset the loss of energy. From what Waylon could tell, Rupert never seemed to tire after sex. Rupert claimed that his energy was depleted the longer he abstained. It seemed to make sense. The one time they'd been unable to stop on a planet inhabited by females for close to a week, Rupert had lain curled in a ball in his quarters. Unsure what to do to aide his friend, Waylon finally gave up and did the only thing he could think of—he hired two girls to try to "cheer" Rupert up. That did the trick. He was up and going full speed by the next morning.

Trinity stirred and moaned softly next to him. He kissed the top of her head lightly and he sighed, knowing he'd have to bid her farewell. Keeping her, while a romantic idea, was insane. They were completely different species and if he ever did find a mate, she'd have to carry human DNA in her. Even though he'd thought to have detected it in her when they first met, the likelihood of her actually having it was slim to none. He'd been so wrapped in lust since first seeing her that he'd probably just misread it.

"Goodbye," he whispered as he slid his arm from around her, steeling his heart for what had to be done. Like it or not, Waylon had to push Trinity away.

* * * * *

Trinity stilled. Someone had touched her. Who? The fog of sleep had yet to lift completely. Never before had she felt this groggy. Not even when she'd woken to find the serial killer on Vedieone standing above her. The drug he'd used was powerful, yet somehow she'd metabolized it quickly. That was one of the reasons the king had wanted her to stay and marry one of his sons. He'd made no bones about her being "special".

Someone nudged her and her RLS-69 training kicked in. Jerking upwards, she took hold of the arm touching her and twisted it madly. Rising to her knees, she prepared to dispose of whoever had dared to touch her. The sight of Waylon's large brown eyes stopped her dead in her track. Dropping his arm quickly, Trinity hung her head.

"I'm sorry. I… I didn't know it was you."

A cold look passed over his face. "I can see how it would be hard for someone in your line of work to remember where you are every morning."

She felt as though she'd been smacked. Too stunned to respond, she merely stared at him, trying to make sense of his turnabout. In the shower, she could have sworn she'd heard Waylon whisper that she was his. If this was how he treated "his property" then she wanted no part of it. Even if she did, she could never act on it. The only man she would ever belong to was Simon. He'd signed for her and assumed control of her fate the day he'd selected her for the RLS-69 program.

Huffing, Trinity yanked away from Waylon and sat on the edge of the bed. "I think now would be the perfect time for me to leave." She knew that her voice sounded hard, cold, just as she had intended it to.

"That may be best," Waylon offered, his tone neutral.

Happy she wasn't facing him, she bit her lower lip in an attempt to push her feelings down deep. She was an expert at hiding her head in the sand and Waylon would just be one more memory she never touched again.

"I don't know where I am but that does happen a lot to *whores* like me. It's also common for us to be thought of as assassins, considering that's what we *all* moonlight as." Each word was clipped as she gritted her teeth.

Waylon touched her back lightly. The heat of his skin, the sting of his words, was too much for her to bear. Leaning forward, Trinity let his hand fall away. She felt a shift of the weight on the bed and knew that Waylon had gotten up. Two could play at this game. She rose to her feet and turned to look at the man who was breaking her heart.

His face was blank. If he did care even a tiny bit about her, he never showed it. It was an expression she used often, especially when facing someone she knew she would hurt or kill. Part of her wanted to prepare for battle, another wanted to give in to the pain in her heart. Thankfully, the fighter in her prevailed.

When he spoke, his voice was guarded and hard. "I'm sorry things got out of hand. It was a case of mistaken identity, that's all. I'll have clothes sent in shortly, since I ruined yours. A vehicle will take you wherever you wish to go."

"That's it?"

It took every bit of power Waylon possessed to turn away from Trinity. His instincts told him to sink his teeth into her flesh as he shot come into her womb but he fought the beast within. On this matter, he'd not give in to that other part of him.

No. The man would prevail.

Waylon focused on the door, knowing his next statement would sever any further communications with Trinity. "Right, sorry I forgot that you're paid to perform. I'll see to it that you are generously compensated for your time and services."

With that, he walked out of the room. His chest was tight and his gut clenched with each step he took down the hall. He had to fight not to run back to her and wrap his arms around her.

Figiutatio mated for life. While Trinity would go on to find someone else, he would forever want only her—a woman he knew nothing about. A woman who sold her body to men. A woman who had been an inmate on Restigatio. A woman who may or may not be a hired assassin.

A woman who now, in the eyes of his people, was considered his wife.

Chapter Six

Trinity sat at the pixeton game table and stared around the casino. It had been days since she'd seen or heard from Waylon and, so far, she hadn't had any luck contacting Simon again.

Thankfully, another encrypted file in her head partially decoded, allowing her to at least read the native Mixlione language. It left her with a hell of a headache for the greater portion of a day but it was worth it. She still wasn't entirely sure about all the colored chips in her bag, but after watching other people interacting, she gathered they were currency. She also knew that Waylon had held true to his promise, he had several bags full of chips dropped off at the hotel she selected along with additional clothing.

She'd been so upset with his presumption that she'd only been with him to be paid that she'd thrown the bags across the hotel room and cried until she could cry no more. The minute she heard herself beg the empty room to make Waylon show up and fix her broken heart with his healing kiss, she came to her senses. She wasn't a beggar. After she'd found a group of thugs trying to rob two old men and beat the living shit out of them. Even that didn't make her feel completely better.

Now, she sat and took in the scene. A raven-haired woman in the corner of the room caught her eye again. It was the third time in the last day that Trinity had found the woman staring at her. She was so familiar yet Trinity couldn't place her. She didn't have a thing against females, but her tastes ran more toward men. So far, the woman had only stared intently at her. An uneasy feeling crept over her but she pushed it down and tore her gaze from the mysterious woman. Never one to let her guard down, Trinity kept her senses heightened just in case something got out of hand.

The A-mac would, or rather should, return her to Restigatio once her mission was complete. The fact that she was still on Mixlione meant that her gut had been right, Waylon was her charge and she was to protect him. Or she'd been wrong and her mission was something altogether different — something connected to Waylon but not directly. Regardless what her actual mission was, Waylon had lit a fire in her she never knew existed. Now, her body ached to be touched and she yearned for release.

A tall man with chin-length jet-black hair caught her eye. There was something familiar about him yet she was positive they'd never met before. The feeling seemed to be running rampant as of late. First the woman and then the handsome man.

Smiling, Trinity lifted her drink and nodded at him. The corner of his mouth pulled up and he made his way across the room to her. He was thin yet looked to be well-defined. In fact, as he got closer, he looked to be more than just well-defined, he was solid. The black suit he wore spoke volumes about his station in life. The man was wealthy. That wasn't a shock. Mixlione seemed to attract the rich and horny.

"Hello. What's a beautiful woman such as yourself doing sitting all alone?" the tall stranger asked, his accent sounding similar to Simon's.

Trinity smiled at him and knew she'd much rather prefer Waylon, but in a pinch this man would do just fine. Since Waylon had turned his back on her and "paid" for her to leave, pinches were all she would ever have. "Does that line work for you often?"

He grabbed his chest and looked slightly taken aback. "Dear lady, you're not implying that I was using some smarmy pickup line, are you?"

"Oh, I'd never imply something like that. It would seriously cut my chances of getting laid tonight."

The man nodded, never breaking his calm exterior. He sat in the seat next to her and tossed a red chip onto the table. "So, you're saying that if I were a betting man, laying odds on the two of us coupling are in my favor then?"

"You could say that."

He smiled. "It's good to find a woman in this place that's interested in a good time and doesn't require payment at the end of the night."

Trinity's gut tightened at the man's words. "What? You don't think I'm a prostitute?"

The man laughed and tossed another chip on the table. "No. I know a prostitute when I see one and trust me, doll, you aren't one. Hot as hell, but definitely not a pay-by-the-hour kind of gal."

"Yeah, well you'd be the first man here to think that. Certain men seem to be fixated on the assumption I am one." There was no hiding the pain in her voice and she knew it. Waylon had worked his way under her defenses and put a hole in her heart. No amount of sexy, well-spoken men would repair the damage. The best she could do now was to enjoy herself while Abbi and Simon tried to get her back to the base. "So, would you like to fuck tonight or not?"

The man paused a moment and then nodded. "Yes, I would. But do you think we should at least get each other's names first?"

Trinity shrugged. "Doesn't matter what you call me just so long as you've got a big dick and are willing to use it."

"Right then, shall we?" he asked, extending his arm to her.

Trinity took it and stood with him. The hairs on the back of her neck stood on end and she turned to find the mysterious brunette watching her. Not able to shake the feeling that she was in danger, Trinity tensed slightly in preparation for battle.

"Are you having second thoughts?"

She smiled up at him. "No. I very much want to fuck my troubles away."

"I'd ask what troubles a beautiful woman like you could have but I get the sense you'd refuse to tell me."

"You've got keen senses."

He chuckled and the sound rolled through her, reminding her of Simon and a bit of Waylon. "That I do, doll. That I do."

They made their way through the casino and headed onto one of the level lifts. Trinity's room was on the fourth level but the tall stranger wasn't going there. No. He pressed the button for the top floor and gave her hand a tiny squeeze.

"I have to admit that I normally don't find brunettes attractive."

Glancing up at him, Trinity laughed. "Yeah, well I normally don't offer to fuck strangers so we're even."

He turned to her and wrapped her in his arms. While it felt good to be held, he wasn't Waylon. Closing her eyes, she found she could easily envision this man as Waylon. Trinity reached up and pulled on the back of his head. When she felt his face near hers, she stood on her tiptoes and puckered her lips.

The stranger's warm breath ran over her, making her body tighten. "I know that you've no desire to share your name with me, but I'm Rupert, in case you wanted to know."

"That's great, Rupert. Now shut up and kiss me."

He did and the moment their tongues touched, Trinity felt an awesome amount of energy pouring through her. Rupert gasped and they both tried to break free from one another but it didn't work. Giving in to the raw sexual energy, Trinity's nipples hardened and she pressed her body against his.

Rupert slid his hand down her body and lifted her tiny red dress. When his hand skated over her hip, Trinity drew in a deep breath. The minute Rupert slid his hand between her thighs and moved her thong aside, she gave in to him. When he inserted his long finger into her pussy, she moaned and rode it hard. He rubbed her clit with his thumb and sent pleasure tingling throughout her body. The combination of the pending orgasm and the power that tore through her made Trinity ride Rupert's fingers even faster.

He pushed his hips against her and she felt him unfastening his dress pants. A second later, the bare head of his cock pressed against her stomach. She moved against it, wishing she was taller so he could fuck her standing up. As much as she wanted to be fucked, she wanted Waylon to be the one in her. It didn't matter. He thought of her as a whore, a hooker to be paid off and never looked at again.

Maybe my uncle was right. Maybe I was destined to be at men's mercy. Maybe a half-breed like me should just lie down on her back and enjoy the ride.

Rupert increased his pace and rubbed her clit faster. Trinity cried out into his mouth as her orgasm hit her. Rupert growled and the power between them flared more. Instantly, her cunt was clenching down on his fingers. He pushed hard against her and came with a start all over her bare stomach. They stayed stuck together, entangled in their own kiss, his throbbing cock against her stomach and his finger in her vagina, until the power within them flickered out.

"What the hell?" Trinity opened her eyes and stared up at Rupert. The shocked looked on his face told her that he was as clueless as she was about the events that had just unfolded.

"You're from Earth or at the very least have Earth blood in your veins," he said, almost in a whisper as he withdrew his fingers from her pussy and straightened her dress.

Trinity cringed and glanced around the level lift nervously. Being human wasn't something you announced publicly. Descendents from the planet Earth had undergone a massive extermination during the Cleansing Wars and were hunted for sport in the hundreds of years since. For humans, that might mean many generations. For some aliens with longer life spans, it meant they were old enough to remember firsthand and they weren't forgetting. Earth was now a ghost planet and what descendents remained kept their identities a secret.

Trinity shook her head and prepared to render Rupert unconscious if need be. "No. Don't be silly. I'm from Salluinic."

Rupert put his cock back in his pants and pressed her against the doors of the level lift. He grabbed her throat gently. Dipping his head down, he licked along her jaw line, making her rub her body against him in response to his touch. His come smeared over her stomach and soaked through the front of her dress. "Shhh, don't be afraid of what you are with me. I'm from Earth as well. I'm a full-blood."

A full-blood?

Trinity froze. That was almost unheard of. Her mother had been a full-blooded Earthling and her father a native of Salluinic. When her parents died, she and her sisters had been sent to live with their uncle. He was a prominent general in the Salluinic army and knew their "family secret".

You're dirty little Earth whores and that's all you'll ever be. Her uncle's words played in her head. She tried to block them out but they kept coming. *I'll not spend my hard-earned money to support dirty lil' whores such as the likes of you three.*

Trinity returned home from school the next day to find her two sisters missing. Her uncle admitted to selling them at the slave auction and he then informed her she was to remain with him and "service his men".

They fight hard for our people. The least you could do is show some respect.

By respect, her uncle had meant lying on her back and spreading her legs. When she'd refused, he had her beaten and chained to the bed. By the grace of the gods, she'd managed to escape. When her uncle found her, days later, hiding in a filthy, rat-infested cave, he'd decided to teach her to respect a man's body personally. The fight that followed left her uncle dead and her hands bloody. Too stunned to move, Trinity had been found by her uncle's troops and sentenced to death on Restigatio for his murder. They didn't care about what he'd tried to force her to do or what he'd almost done to her. No, the fact that she'd refused to obey a male in her family only made her sentence more severe.

Her uncle's attempts at making her a prostitute for his armies was the reason Trinity had taken Waylon's paying her for her "performance" so hard. It was also the reason Simon had made it clear that she in no way was expected to sleep with any men on her missions. As horrific as her life had been, it was because of that she'd even met Simon and Abbi. She had the ability to kill in her, yet Simon told her again and again that her heart was pure. Trinity wasn't so sure about that.

Rupert touched her forehead and the memories of her uncle dissipated quickly. Trinity stared up at him with wide eyes. "What did you do to me?"

"I'm sorry, doll. I didn't know you were part Earthling or I'd have never touched you without increasing my metaphysical shields."

"Metaphysical what...?" The level lift doors opened suddenly and Trinity tumbled backward, taking Rupert with her.

They landed in a heap on the hallway floor. Rupert's body was planted firmly over hers in the missionary position. He gave her a sheepish smile and put his forehead against hers. "Ah, it's good to find another like us."

"Us?" Trinity asked, making no attempt to get up. While Rupert was no Waylon, he did make her feel safe and that was something that didn't happen often. To date, Simon and Waylon had been the only other men in her life to have ever made her feel that way. One man owned her life while the other owned her heart.

Rupert's pale blue eyes flickered to violet and then swirled back to blue. He brought the hand he'd fingered her with to his mouth and inserted it, licking her come from it and rubbing his hips against her body. Something passed over Rupert's face and he withdrew her fingers from his mouth. "You're mated?"

Trinity stayed frozen in place beneath him, still shocked by the trick he'd done with his eyes. Waylon's eyes had done something similar. "You're a *figiutatio*."

It was Rupert's turn to freeze. "What...? How...?"

"Rupert, you had better be here because I just ran up two hundred flights of stairs to get to you. Something is wrong with the level lifts. One is stuck and the other one is being serviced now... What the hell?"

The sound of Waylon's voice made Trinity look up. He stood above them, dressed in dark gray pants and a white dress shirt. He clutched a matching gray jacket in his hand. Trinity's gaze inched up his muscular body and when she reached his face, she found it hard, void of emotion.

"Waylon?" she whispered, still shocked to see him.

Rupert stared down at her, his eyes wide. "You know Waylon?" Trinity nodded and Rupert closed his eyes, appearing to be in pain. He sighed. "How exactly do you know him? Please tell me that he's not your mate."

Trinity's body tightened. She spoke to Rupert but glared at Waylon, "Uhh, no. He's not my mate. He's the guy who assumed I was a prostitute and paid me after my *performance* was over then walked away without so much as a goodbye. But that wasn't before he accused me of trying to kill him."

A feral look came over Waylon as he leered down at them. "Guess I wasn't far off the mark. Tell me, Trinity, what elaborate scheme did you use to seduce Rupert? The men attacking you in the alley were a nice touch. You didn't reuse the same lame-ass skit again, did you? Please don't tell me that you've burned your way through all that money I paid you."

Rupert rolled off her fast and pulled her to her feet. "Trinity? Your name is Trinity? Shit, you're not *the* Trinity are you? You're not *his* Trinity, right?"

Disgusted, Trinity put her hand on her hip and glared at both of them. "No. I'm not his anything. Goodbye, gentlemen. I wish you both the best in whatever the hell it is the two of you do!" She turned to leave.

"See, there's where you're wrong, Trinity." The anger in Waylon's voice made her pause. "Not only are you *my* Trinity, you're *my* wife."

Trinity laughed hard but didn't turn around. She couldn't face him. Facing him would force her to admit that she loved him and that she'd hurt him. It wasn't something she could do.

"I can't be your wife, Waylon. For one, we never got married and for two, killer prostitutes don't have husbands." Trinity didn't wait to hear his response. Instead, she stormed down the long hallway and didn't stop until she found the staff level lift. It would be tiny and lack any great features, but it'd get her where she needed to go—away from Waylon.

Waylon watched Trinity walking away from him but he made no move to stop her. The hurt, the betrayal he felt when he found her lying beneath his best friend was too much for him to deal with. The second he saw her smiling up at Rupert, he knew that he'd not only mated himself to her, he'd fallen in love with her too.

"I didn't know you were mated to her," Rupert said, his voice low. He shook his head slightly and rubbed between his eyes. It was something he did often after falling too deep into someone else's mind.

Had he been in Trinity's thoughts? The idea of that made another pang of jealousy rip through Waylon.

"Spill it, Rupert. What the hell is going on?"

"I swear I didn't know she was your Trinity. I didn't "get" that from her before we…before I accidentally…well, we…"

"Spit it out!"

"I didn't know she was your wife before I touched her."

Waylon gave him a droll look and clutched his jacket tighter. "Yeah, you've already said that."

"You do not understand what I'm trying to tell you, Waylon. I couldn't help myself. I saw her from across the casino and thought she was the most beautiful woman I'd ever seen. When she told me that she just wanted to spend the night fucking away her troubles, I couldn't say no. I…I…wanted to do exactly that for her. I wanted to take away the hurt in her eyes, the sorrow I felt in her heart."

Red hot rage tore through Waylon. Instantly, the beast within him tried to surface. He managed to control it but failed to control the human side. Quickly, he seized hold of Rupert's throat and slammed him against the hallway wall, pushing him almost all the way through it. Rupert made no attempt to protect himself and that was the only thing that kept Waylon sane enough not to kill his best friend.

"She asked you to fuck her?" Waylon demanded. The idea of Trinity begging another man to touch her sickened him.

Rupert tried to answer but the grip on his throat was too tight. Waylon eased the pressure a bit. "Yes, but I could feel that she cared for another…that she might possibly even be in love with that person. And I swear that I had no clue it was you when we entered the lift. When I kissed her, my power broke loose and encircled us wildly before it flowed directly through us. I tried to break away, so did she, but nothing worked. I had to touch her. I couldn't help myself."

Hearing Rupert's explanation did little in the way of calming his nerves. Waylon still wanted to kill him, but he didn't. He stayed still and took several deep breaths. Something Rupert had mentioned struck him and he narrowed his gaze on his longtime friend. "You said that she cared for someone else…that she might even love that person. Did you see who the person was?"

"No. I only saw an image of her in a room throwing bags of money chips against the wall and crying. When she thought of this, I heard her pleading with no one in particular for the man to return even long enough to just fix her broken heart with his healing kisses."

Waylon's heart soared. Rupert had to be talking about him. He'd been unable to stop himself from kissing Trinity's wrist once he'd seen the abrasion he'd caused on her perfect skin. The heat from his healing magic had flared through him once more and mended her.

"My wife loves me," he whispered, sounding foolish even to himself. He let go of Rupert and headed down the hall.

"Where are you going?"

Waylon turned and smiled at his friend. "To find my wife. And I fully plan on kicking the shit out of you later for touching her."

Instantly, Rupert's magic slammed into him and held him to his spot. "I'm sorry, Waylon, but I can't let you do that."

"Come on. What the hell are you doing? Trinity is getting further away each second I delay. I need to find her, Rupert. I need to make this right with my mate. I accused her of…of things I should have never thought, let alone said aloud. I need to make this right. You know as well as I do how rare it is for our people to find a mate."

Rupert sighed. "I do know how hard it is for our people to find a mate. But I saw something else when I read her, I saw someone close to her dying. You're her mate and that leaves you the prime target."

Waylon chuckled. "Have you not heard a single word I've said? The woman I love is getting away. I don't give a shit if I'm hurt or not. Hell, someone took enough shots at me the other night to rip me to shreds, yet here I am."

"She's going to die too, Waylon. I sensed imminent danger all around her."

"No…gods no, Rupert. Let me up! I can't let anything happen to her." Waylon felt Rupert's hesitation and then the conflict in him. It hit him then. "Oh my gods! You bound her to you too!"

Rupert nodded and Waylon lashed out against his power. The energy holding him ripped at him, forcing him to his knees.

This was a fighting tactic he'd seen Rupert use hundreds of years ago, during the Cleansing Wars. It wasn't something he'd ever thought would be directed at him.

"How could you bind her to you, Rupert? How? She's my wife. My mate."

"Not the extent you did, but we formed a bond. As much as I want to keep her safe, I want you alive more. Why the hell didn't you mark her? I would have smelled you on her if you'd have just bitten her. I wouldn't have seen all of those horrible events of her past and I wouldn't have sensed that death was near."

Waylon cursed himself. Rupert was right. If he'd have just taken that next step and sunk his teeth into her flesh, she'd have worn his scent for the rest of eternity. But he'd refused.

Rupert laughed. "Oh, I get it. Because you 'assumed' she was a prostitute and that made her beneath you. You'd never willingly tie yourself to a whore. Is that it? Too bad she isn't one or you'd have some merit to your claim. Even if she was, Waylon, it shouldn't matter. If you truly love someone, you look past everything and only see her."

Waylon looked away, ashamed of himself. "What the hell was I supposed to think? You sent her to me and all you *ever* send me is hookers. How was I to know Trinity was different? That she was special? She shows up, kicks the crap out of five men, saves me from taking a sniper phaser blast to the head and starts spitting out the words assassination and *figiutatio*. How the hell does she even know we exist?"

"Like I said, you thought she was beneath you. You've always been a prick who is used to having things your way and it… Wait a minute. Did you just say that I sent her to you?"

Waylon rolled his eyes and pushed hard against Rupert's magic. It didn't break. "Yes. Trinity was right where you said she'd be, by my vehicle. And she matched your description to a tee."

Rupert shook his head and looked panicked. "No. Trinity is *not* the girl I sent for you. The girl I sent you *is* a prostitute who approached me shortly after we landed a couple of weeks ago. She's nothing I'd find sexy. A little too rough around the edges for my taste. I suppose other men would find her alluring, even captivating, but not me."

"Trinity isn't the girl you sent for me?"

"Apparently, my magic is making you deaf as well as dumb." Rupert moved closer to him. "No! Trinity isn't the girl I sent to you!"

"Then how'd she know about the *figiutatio*?"

"My guess is that Simon told her."

The very mention of Trinity's "Simon" made his blood boil. He glared at Rupert. "Yeah, her little Simon is a real winner."

Rupert bent down next to him and shook his head. "Waylon, you've always been a hot head. You immediately assume the worst about the man because you finally got a hard-on over a woman. Her Simon is our Simon, you idiot!" Rupert leaned in closer. "You know, Simon Thornton, head of the fourth legion of *figiutatio* during the uprising. Son of one of the greatest rulers we'd ever known."

Waylon seized hold of Rupert and pinned him to the ground, instantly breaking his magic. "Great, I'm an idiot with a hot temper and you are a jackass who was always shit when it came to fighting maneuvers. Guess it's a good thing you were a sorcerer and a physic, not a warrior, or we would have never survived."

He rolled off Rupert and pulled his defenses up. Rupert could attack now and Waylon would be ready for him.

"I am going to find my wife," he growled. "If anything has happened to her I'll hold you accountable, friend or not!"

"She's not your wife anymore. My bond with her will prevent you from marking her. I won't release her, Waylon! I'll not be party to your death." Rupert stood next to him and he waited for another round of fighting to ensue. None did.

"She won't be anyone's wife if we don't find her soon. There's something dark in her, something that I get the sense is going to come to a head very soon. Are you sure about the death thing? Even your powers get muddled up."

Rupert sighed and Waylon glanced back at him. When he met his friend's pale blue gaze, he could tell Rupert knew exactly what the darkness Trinity harbored was. He'd find Trinity and save her himself, keeping Rupert out of the line of fire. It had been many, many years since they'd fought in battle and they weren't as young as they used to be.

Chapter Seven

Trinity stared at herself in the mirror. Her hair was soaked from her shower and the towel she held around her body covered more than any of the dresses she'd worn over the last few days, but she still felt naked. Waylon's words had stripped her down, exposed old wounds she'd thought had long since healed.

Being subjected to her uncle's wrath and hatred had left part of her heart dark, so dark that nothing would ever penetrate it. How a man who'd fathered a half-human child himself could hate them so much was unknown to her. The child and her mother fled shortly after she was born. The only reason Trinity knew about it was because she'd overheard some of his men discussing it. Robbie, Roberta, damn, now Trinity couldn't remember the child's name.

Someone knocked on her hotel room door. "Go away. I don't want to be disturbed!"

"Excuse me, ma'am, but you have a message from a Mr. Waylon…"

"Hold on," Trinity shouted, not letting the woman finish her sentence. She shouldn't care what Waylon had to say. Hell, he probably sent her a message to tell her how much of a whore she was.

Trinity flung the door open and instantly flew backward. Pain moved through her insides and she hit the floor with a thud. It felt as though someone had struck her in the chest with a moving transport vehicle. Every muscle in her body burned as she tried to stand. Instantly, her body lit with an inner fire, keeping her pinned to her spot a moment.

"Fool! I knew you wouldn't be able to resist that one," the woman said as she moved over her.

Trinity recognized the woman. She was the raven-haired beauty from the casino, the one who'd been watching her. Her eyes widened when she saw the P341 firephaser she was holding. Had the woman shot her with that? If the woman had, then Trinity was living on borrowed time. A hit from one of those was fatal, regardless of the amount of juice behind it.

The woman looked puzzled for a moment as her brow furrowed and her eyes narrowed. "There's something...familiar about you."

Trinity's body began to cramp and she knew that she had to move to keep her blood pumping. The P341s were at their worst when the victim lay still. She rolled to her side and cried out as the woman above her kicked her side.

"Nice try, agent."

"Agent?" Trinity asked as her chest burned.

"Yeah, I was hired to bring you back to Vedieone and that's exactly what I plan on doing. The king wasn't very specific on what sort of shape you needed to be in." The woman laughed. "I get to dispose of your lover-boy too. Turns out the king's head sorcerer read your future when he "blessed you" and saw you marrying Waylon. It made it easy for me to locate you—the minute the sorcerer said he saw you outside a casino, I knew to come here."

Trinity tried to stand again and failed. "But...why...?"

"Agent girl, they'll take anyone into that program, won't they? Good gods, the King of Vedieone offered one of his many sons to you and you rejected him. That, my dear, is the ultimate insult. The second the head sorcerer reported that you would end up here, marry Waylon and carry his child, the king's fury bordered on out of control. That's when he called me in. I get to kill your husband and drag your ass back to marry the son of your choice. Though, if you are with child, I'm guessing they'll take care of that. Wouldn't want to spoil the royal bloodline or anything."

"Get away from her!" Waylon shouted.

"No!" Trinity didn't want his help. The woman had already said she'd been ordered to execute him. Scared for Waylon's life, Trinity mustered all her strength and swept the woman's legs out from under her. Her weapon discharged and hit Trinity in the leg. Instantly, the effects of the poisonous phaser riddled through her system. Waylon cried out and the next thing she knew, he had her wrapped in his arms.

"I don't think so," Rupert yelled from across the room.

There was a bright flash of white-blue light and the assassin screamed out. Waylon looked down into her eyes and hugged her close to him. "I'm so sorry, honey. I was afraid of what I felt for you. I didn't know love when it damn near slit my throat with its pumps. Please forgive me."

Trinity forced a smile and stroked Waylon's cheek lightly. Seeing his face, she couldn't help but say, "I love you, Waylon."

Waylon's face scrunched up as if in pain. "I love you too, baby."

Rupert appeared next to her and grabbed hold of the sides of her head. Waylon nodded. A second before the darkness swallowed her, she thought she heard Simon's voice.

"Allow me to assist."

Waylon turned and found Simon Thornton standing in the entrance way with a tall blond man. He glanced at Rupert for his opinion but Rupert was heavy into the healing process with Trinity.

Simon's gaze darted to the floor to the assassin. "Ah, I take it you are Callida, universal gun for hire."

"How do you know who I am?" Callida's round eyes glanced over them all like they were crazy.

"Easy, Prince Makken from Vedieone arrived on Restigatio and informed me of his father's plan." Simon touched the man's shoulder next to him. "He was strongly opposed to his father's idea and immediately sought to warn Trinity. She of course was already here. It is bad enough that her own uncle turned against her but to have another blood relative do the same is unimaginable. Trinity has only been guilty of loving others too much and fighting to protect herself. That in no way makes her deserve this."

"Trinity?" the woman asked in disbelief. "Oh gods, she looked so familiar to me. No. It can't be her. That's impossible. The odds are...she can't be. No, not my Trinity."

Waylon glared down at her. "She's not your anything and mark my words, after Rupert heals her, I'm going to kill you."

Callida's eyes filled with tears as she stared past him to Trinity. "I didn't know. I haven't seen her in almost twenty years."

"Let this be a lesson, Callida," Simon murmured softly, "to learn more about your targets than their job title. Had you bothered to learn her name, you may have thought twice about poisoning your own sister. A sister who killed your uncle to avoid being given to his armies for their sexual satisfaction, a woman who spent years in a hard prison facility, fighting to stay alive in all the madness until I found her. A sister who was sent on this assignment to meet her husband, her mate, and to be reunited with her long-lost family. And a woman that I care deeply about. I will even venture far enough to say that I love her. She is my friend and I do not take kindly to her being harmed in any way."

The room was quiet as Rupert continued to work on Trinity.

Chapter Eight

"Simon, are you sure that our Trinity will be fine?" Abbi asked as he walked past her viewing screen.

Simon glanced over to Rupert and bit back a smile as he saw the stunned look on the man's face. "She looks identical to…"

"Yes, I know. It's my way of honoring her. Even in death, she's remembered."

Abbi tipped her head to the side, sending long black waves of hair over her shoulder. "Rupert's DNA is closely related to yours, as is Waylon's. Why is this?"

"They are like me, Abbi, and now they are part of the mission. You may speak freely in front of either of them. Rupert will be staying with us to aid with the program and Waylon and Trinity are moving to the first of the outside settlements on the planet here to live and await the birth of their first child. Her sister will remain in solitary confinement until I deem it appropriate to begin her RLS training. Trinity wishes no harm to come to her, nor do I. Callida is punishing herself enough for a hundred men."

"So Trinity will be close enough to visit?"

"Not only that, Abbi. She and Waylon have agreed to help with the RLS program as well. So she will be with us often, as a member of the team, not a prisoner so you may speak freely in front of her as well."

"My sensors are most pleased."

"Sensors are pleased?" Rupert asked, laughing slightly.

Simon shot his longtime friend a look and he stopped laughing.

"Simon," Abbi said. "Agent Roberta is awaiting entrance."

"Send her in."

Simon watched as Bobbie entered. Today's drab clothing was a large gray T-shirt and sweatpants. Her cap covered her eyes and her posture was anything but ladylike.

"You wanted to see me, sir?" Bobbie didn't bother to look around.

"It's Simon, Bobbie." Simon sighed. "We've been over this before."

Rupert coughed, choking back another laugh. "Umm, Simon, you told me that this place was full of women. Are you sure you didn't make some sort of mistake?"

Simon bit his lip as Bobbie lifted her cap, revealing her emerald green eyes, and glared at Rupert. "Funny, as far as I knew this place was an asshole-free zone. Guess I was wrong."

Glancing at Rupert, Simon nearly fell over laughing when he found his friend's mouth hanging open. It looked like he was shocked by Bobbie's words, but Simon knew better.

"Yes, Bobbie, I wanted to inform you that you'll be aiding Rupert with self-defense and weapons training from here on out. Since Trinity is now expecting and has already had undo stress put on her and the child, I do not think it's wise for her to continue on in that manner. Besides, her services are needed behind the scenes."

Bobbie's eyes widened. "You can't seriously expect a pretty boy like Mr. Saturday Night over there to know how to fight." Bobbie glanced at the viewing screen and smiled. "I'm diggin' those late-night lessons, Abbi."

"As am I, Roberta."

Rupert closed the distance between them fast and it was all Simon could do just to keep a straight face. "I'll have you know, Ms. Tomboy, I am skilled enough when it comes to hand-to-hand combat, though if you asked Waylon he'd disagree. And I am an expert on weapons and technology. Though, by the looks of your outfit, you don't really care to be with the times."

Bobbie spun around fast, tossed her leg in the air and kicked Rupert square in the chest. He staggered backward and almost fell onto the floor. Bobbie stared at Simon. "I'll report to the holding cell and inform them I'll be staying awhile this time. Teaching that arrogant snob a lesson was worth it though."

Simon hid his smile under his hand until it passed. "No, Bobbie, I'll let this one slide. Please go and find Gillian. Britney tells me that she ran out during the "how to properly use a dildo" lesson again today and has not been seen since."

"No surprise there," Bobbie bit out, spinning on her heels and leaving the room.

"Sorry about Bobbie, Rupert, but she's a stubborn one."

"Yeah, I noticed. Is she always that high-strung?" Rupert rubbed his chest where he was kicked, staring at the door.

Simon smiled. He knew Rupert wasn't really hurt. Bobbie could've kicked him a lot harder if she wanted to. Rupert, being what he was, could've taken it. No, the look on Rupert's face was more shock that she actually did kick him more than anything. "You know what they say — *Amour ōdit inertēs*."

"What the hell does cupid hating the lazy have to do with this?" Rupert finally pried his eyes away from the door and frowned.

Simon tipped his head and looked away. "You'll see soon enough, old friend. Now, what do you say we go talk to Prince Makken before he departs? After, you can tour the RLS facility. Hmm, maybe Bobbie could show you around."

Tossing his hands in the air, Rupert stalked out of the door mumbling about how he only signed up because he was promised beautiful women agents but was only finding rude ones. Simon turned and looked at Abbi. Even she looked amused.

"We did good, Abbi. All three agents found their mates and all three are with child."

"It's begun."

"Yes, it has begun."

"Simon?"

"Yes, Abbi, what is it?"

Abbi worried her lip. "Since Trinity's husband is immortal, what will happen to them since she's mortal?"

Simon shook his head slightly. Abbi really was getting more and more perceptive and even more curious. He wasn't sure if it was a bad thing or not. Regardless, he wouldn't change it.

"She's not mortal anymore, Abbi. When they mated, Waylon gave part of himself to her and now she and her baby will be like the rest of us. In fact all of the women will become like their husbands in time. It's a natural side-effect of the mating process."

"That is just so romantic." Abbi grinned, dabbing at her teary eyes. "I want to have a baby too, Simon."

Simon cleared his throat and ignored Abbi's declaration. "Prepare the A-mac for additional agent transfers. I don't think we should wait any longer than we need to."

"Yes, Simon. I will begin preparations immediately. Who will we be sending out?"

Simon smiled. "Gillian, Dahlia and Bobbie."

"Simon, I thought that Bobbie's mate was…"

He put his hand up, silencing Abbi. "Just do as I ask please."

"Yes, Simon."

The End

About Mandy M. Roth

I grew up fascinated by creatures that go bump in the night. From the very beginning I was odd and creative — a combo every mother hopes for. After studying art all the way through school, I majored in it at college. One rather unexpected child later, I changed my major and finished with a great balance of art and business. I'm working on my MBA with a concentration in marketing but it's taken a back seat while I plug away at the keyboard.

I live in Ohio with my husband and three boys. They definitely keep me busy. Between convincing one he really doesn't need to have his eyebrow pierced, listening to the middle one's philosophy on life and pulling the youngest off the countertop, I do manage to eek in a very small amount of writing time during the day. More often than not, my writing is done from 8pm until 3 am.

If the following years are half as good as my first one in writing, I'll be a happy gal! I'm doing something I love, meeting tons of new people, have the greatest readers in the world and the support of my family. The only thing I still don't have is that hot lycan on a motorcycle. I'm working on it, though.

Mandy welcome mail from readers. You can write to them c/o Ellora's Cave Publishing at 1056 Home Avenue, Akron OH 44310-3502.

About Michelle M. Pillow

Born and still living in the Midwest, Michelle M Pillow has always had an active imagination. Ever since she can remember, she's had a strange fascination with anything supernatural— ghosts, magical powers, and oh...vampires. What could be more alluring than being immortal, all-powerful, and eternally beautiful? After discovering historical romance novels in high school, it was only natural that the supernatural and romance elements should someday meet in her wonderland of a brain. She's glad they did, for their children have been pouring onto the computer screen ever since.

She fell madly in love with and married a tattoo artist/body piercer, who is her personal "knight in colorful armor". They own a successful tattoo and body piercing studio. Her vivacious daughter and loving husband constantly attempt to plague her home with new pets. So far they've managed to get two prairie dogs, countless fish, two cats, a dog and one African Grey parrot past her guard—at least, that is all she has seen so far.

Michelle would love to hear from you and tries to answer her emails in a timely fashion. That is if the current hero will let her go long enough to check the computer.

Michelle welcome mail from readers. You can write to them c/o Ellora's Cave Publishing at 1056 Home Avenue, Akron OH 44310-3502.

Also by Mandy M. Roth & Michelle M. Pillow

Pleasure Cruise

Enjoy this excerpt from

Pleasure Cruise

© Copyright Mandy M. Roth and

Michelle M. Pillow 2005

Interoffice Memo
From: The Powers That Be
Re: Pleasure Cruise, Cruise Line Corporation, Pilot Program
TOP SECRET

Due to the dwindling population of certain supernatural factions and the reluctance of the supernatural kind to take mates for all eternity, we will be establishing a comprehensive program to repopulate the various supernatural species. Many of the supernaturals we've observed are unwilling to take mates from within their own population. This reluctance has been exacerbated in large part by the old grudges still held from the Middle Ages.

In an unprecedented move, we will now be allowing humans on the Pleasure Cruise, to participate in the preordained mating process. Because of existing prejudices against supernaturals in human culture, some human participants will not be aware of the paranormal elements on the cruise. However, these humans will be blessed with a sixth sense so as to subconsciously recognize their mate upon first sight. We do not wish to have a boat full of frightened humans defying our will. Some resistance is expected, but in the end, we gods know what's best for them.

It is our hope that, by introducing humans into their bloodlines, the supernatural will be less reluctant to take a mate. All humans who mate themselves to a supernatural will be blessed with eternal life. They will also be given the gift of procreation. If this goes well, we will be slowly introducing humans into our other business ventures as well, including Pleasure Air and Pleasure Island.

* * * * *

Clare grimaced as she looked at the gangway of the cruise ship and took a deep breath, trying to steel herself to get on board. A long strand of wavy, blonde hair worked itself out of her loose ponytail. Kira had talked her into the highlights and every time she saw them it caused her to pause. Frowning, she pushed the lock out of her face and reached down to grab her duffel bag. Slinging the bag over her shoulder, she looked around. This wasn't something she'd ever imagined herself doing. No, she was a career-driven woman who never thought of anything beyond deadlines and new deals. Clare was still shocked she'd agreed to this trip.

"Welcome to the boat of love. I wonder what will happen on this week's exciting journey? Will the captain steer the boat off course and into a giant iceberg? Or will the tired executive toss herself overboard due to lack of intellectual stimulation?" she muttered, a little too sarcastically.

"That was the *Titanic* that hit the iceberg. And for the record, I graduated with honors…summa cum laude, baby. And I'd gloat but you graduated with the same honorable distinction," her best friend, Kira, answered, smiling.

"I know. If you recall, I was there. Besides, I wasn't implying that you weren't intelligent. Though I am happy to see that you've decided to admit you're smart. Why you always feel the need to hide it is beyond me," Clare said. "You're the top of your field. You should be proud of it, not ashamed."

"I'm not ashamed. I just don't want to be labeled as some boring pinstripe workaholic prude because I happen to be good at my job. I hate stereotypes."

"We've already agreed to disagree on this topic. Because I love you like a sister I'll let it drop." Clare did her best to smile.

"Thank you," Kira answered, grinning. "I don't complain about your boring life and you don't complain about my wild one."

"Kira…"

"Okay, dropped." Kira winked.

"This is just very different for me. I spent my life avoiding these types of getaways only to find myself here now. Besides, can't a girl be left in her nice little pessimistic place?" Clare grumbled. "Even you have to agree that drowning might be preferable to learning how to play shuffleboard."

Kira laughed and winked. "Yes, I totally agree about the shuffleboard thing. Besides, with my lack of grace I'd only end up slipping in front of the world's sexiest man. Hopefully, he'd be a lawyer. Then he'd want to talk to me about a possible lawsuit. We could discuss it over a lovely night of screwing."

"Kira!" Clare scolded.

Tossing her hands in the air, Kira snickered. "Just kidding. But thanks for taking on the stern mother role you do so well."

"Someone has to try to keep you in line."

Why an electronic book?

We live in the Information Age—an exciting time in the history of human civilization in which technology rules supreme and continues to progress in leaps and bounds every minute of every hour of every day. For a multitude of reasons, more and more avid literary fans are opting to purchase e-books instead of paperbacks. The question to those not yet initiated to the world of electronic reading is simply: *why?*

1. *Price.* An electronic title at Ellora's Cave Publishing and Cerridwen Press runs anywhere from 40-75% less than the cover price of the <u>exact same title</u> in paperback format. Why? Cold mathematics. It is less expensive to publish an e-book than it is to publish a paperback, so the savings are passed along to the consumer.

2. *Space.* Running out of room to house your paperback books? That is one worry you will never have with electronic novels. For a low one-time cost, you can purchase a handheld computer designed specifically for e-reading purposes. Many e-readers are larger than the average handheld, giving you plenty of screen room. Better yet, hundreds of titles can be stored within your new library—a single microchip. (Please note that Ellora's Cave and Cerridwen Press does not endorse any specific brands. You can check our website at www.ellorascave.com or

www.cerridwenpress.com for customer recommendations we make available to new consumers.)

3. *Mobility.* Because your new library now consists of only a microchip, your entire cache of books can be taken with you wherever you go.

4. *Personal preferences are accounted for.* Are the words you are currently reading too small? Too large? Too...**ANNOYING**? Paperback books cannot be modified according to personal preferences, but e-books can.

5. *Instant gratification.* Is it the middle of the night and all the bookstores are closed? Are you tired of waiting days—sometimes weeks—for online and offline bookstores to ship the novels you bought? Ellora's Cave Publishing sells instantaneous downloads 24 hours a day, 7 days a week, 365 days a year. Our e-book delivery system is 100% automated, meaning your order is filled as soon as you pay for it.

Those are a few of the top reasons why electronic novels are displacing paperbacks for many an avid reader. As always, Ellora's Cave and Cerridwen Press welcomes your questions and comments. We invite you to email us at service@ellorascave.com, service@cerridwenpress.com or write to us directly at: 1056 Home Ave. Akron OH 44310-3502.

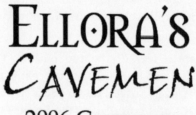

N<small>EED</small> <small>A</small> <small>MORE</small> EXCITING
W<small>AY</small> <small>TO</small> P<small>LAN</small> <small>YOUR</small> D<small>AY</small>?

E<small>LLORA'S</small>
C<small>AVEMEN</small>
2006 C<small>ALENDAR</small>

C<small>OMING</small> T<small>HIS</small> F<small>ALL</small>

THE
ELLORA'S CAVE
LIBRARY

Stay up to date with Ellora's Cave Titles
in Print with our Quarterly Catalog.

TO RECIEVE A CATALOG,
SEND AN EMAIL WITH YOUR NAME
AND MAILING ADDRESS TO:

CATALOG@ELLORASCAVE.COM

OR SEND A LETTER OR POSTCARD
WITH YOUR MAILING ADDRESS TO:
CATALOG REQUEST
C/O ELLORA'S CAVE PUBLISHING, INC.
1337 COMMERCE DRIVE #13
STOW, OH 44224

Discover for yourself why readers can't get enough of the multiple award-winning publisher Ellora's Cave. Whether you prefer e-books or paperbacks, be sure to visit EC on the web at www.ellorascave.com for an erotic reading experience that will leave you breathless.

www.ellorascave.com